FAMILY FIRST

FAMILY FIRST
THE MOTTO

MOMASON WRIGHT

Library of Congress Control Number:		2020924863
ISBN:	Hardcover	978-1-6641-5341-7
	Softcover	978-1-6641-5340-0
	eBook	978-1-6641-5339-4

Print information available on the last page.

Rev. date: 01/19/2021

To order additional copies of this book, contact:
Xlibris
844-714-8691
www.Xlibris.com
Orders@Xlibris.com
819352

Thank You

First and foremost, I thank the man above because
he gave me the talent to think and write as I do.
I thank you, Sherrial Wright-Smtih. You just don't
know, woman—words cannot and will not express it.
You can rest in heaven tho, because I'm in yo bag.

I thank my father, Charles Starks. I am you all over
again. I love you. To my children, regardless if I don't
come around or be around, I want you to know that I
love you. I do what I do so you won't ever struggle.

Jaw's . . . too many to name. That means we are here.

Put your name on the line below if I left you out.

_____

Family First
The
Motto

SPECIAL THANKS

To my wife, I know I have made mistake after mistake, yet
you have been by my side. I can go on about everything
you have done and been through dealing with me.

Yet I would rather take this moment to give
you, Tyronta D. Wright, your flowers because
you deserve them and much more.
Shoutout to Diron, Shawn, Tasha, Meka, and Conrad,
my siblings on my daddy's side, to many to name.

*

I love you—always have and always will

*

Introduction

The smell of blood and the sound of gunshots were still ringing out loud and clear. Most children can still remember the gifts that they received for their birthday, but not Duke. All he could remember was Mayham, and the look of death.

When he heard the door come crashing down, he ran and hid under the bed. The thought of waking his father did run across his mind, but Duke was too scared to move. For a moment, he thought that the men were police because they were the only ones that he knew with guns that big. He watched one of the men put a gun to his father's head.

"What that—"

"I'm only gonna ask you one time, nigga. Where the money and dope."

The bedroom light came on, and he had to watch his mother be manhandled. The house grew silent, and the air became as thick as a block of cement. Before Big Duke could respond, the men snatched him out of the bed and began to pistol-whip him. Duke could hear what sounded like bones cracking as the guns came crashing down on top of his father's head. He wanted to scream when his father fell to the floor, but the look on his face told Duke not to open his mouth.

"You think a nigga playing wit you, huh," one of the men stated.

They beat his father until they realize that he wasn't going to give them what they came for. It was either kill them and find it themselves, or try a different method. The head man look down at Cher on the bed and saw a way to get what he wanted.

"I thought that you was smarter than this, ole head. I don't usually do what I'm about to do, but you got me outside of my character right now."

Duke couldn't see what was going on, but he could put two and two together. Cher began to kick and wiggle her legs, but she was no match for the masked men. Her panties were ripped off, stuffed down her throat, and tape was placed over her mouth.

"You can stop this," he assured Big Duke. "Give me what I came for, and we gone leave."

Big Duke didn't respond, and the masked man let his pants fall down to his ankles. He lay on top of Cher and forced his way inside of her.

"We gone fuck this pretty bitch until the sun comes up," he stated, pushing deep inside of Cher as he pulled her hair.

Big Duke tried to close his eyes and drop his head, but he was forced to watch it take place. Every time his head dropped, it was lifted back up. When he closed his eyes, a pistol was slammed down on top of his head until he reopened them. The lead man put a gun to Cher's head and made her suck his dick. The second man stood up to get behind Cher as she gave the lead man head, but Big Duke stopped him.

"It's in the deep freezer, inside of the waffle boxes."

One of the men left the room and came back a few moments later, eating a Popsicle, holding a garbage bag full. Duke peeped from under the bed and saw one of the men screwing something on to the end of the gun in his hand.

"It's nice doing bidness, ole head."

Big Duke fell to the floor with a glassy look in his eyes, blood pouring from the dime-sized hole in his forehead. Duke knew something was wrong. He waited until the men ran out of the house before coming out from under the bed. His young mind couldn't, wouldn't, and didn't want to register what had taken place. He sat on the floor, in a pool of blood beside his father, and grabbed the cordless phone.

"Hello," a sleepy voice answered.

"Auntie, they want get up."

"Who . . . Duke, it's—" She roll over to look at the bedside clock. "It's four in the morning, where the hell is yo daddy at?"

"He lay right here, but—"

"Boy, put yo dam daddy on the phone."

"Him and Moma bleeding . . . They want get up."

The phone went dead in his ear, and Duke set it down. He couldn't tell whether he was coming or going, and who could at his age. He did what any ten-year-old would do: Duke climbed up onto the bed and fell asleep beside his mother.

*   *   *   *   *

It would be a lie to say that he hadn't thought about suicide after being shuffled from orphanage to orphanage. Duke's eyes were focused out the window as the Greyhound bus turn down the I-20 exit ramp.

"Welcome to Monroe, Louisiana. We will be having a three-hour layover for those of you who will be tagging along, and for the rest of you, have a nice day."

Duke was the first person to plant a foot on solid ground, looking around, letting his eyes take in the scenery. After sucking in a breath of fresh air, he grabbed the bags from under the bus and flagged down a cab. As if on cue, the cabdriver drove right through his childhood neighborhood. Memories normally began to flood his mind. The more Duke began to reminisce, the more he wanted to break down and cry.

"You OK, kid," he asked, pulling up to a house sitting on the corner.

"This my stop."

"Yea, but—"

"How much the meter say?" Duke asked, cutting him off.

"11.50."

"Here, keep the change," Duke told him, dropping two ten-dollar bills on the seat.

He made it halfway up the driveway, and the screen door flew open. Aunt Roz ran to him with open arms.

"Ohh, you done got so big," she told him, taking a step back. "An you looking just like yo daddy."

Duke opened his mouth to speak, but his words were somewhere inside of his stomach. The tears came steamrolling down his cheeks before he could stop them.

"Why you do me like that?"

"Wha . . . what's wrong?" she drooled in regretfully.

"Don't act like you don't know what I'm talking about. Let them take me away and didn't even try to come get me."

"Don't come—"

Duke threw his hand up so fast she thought that he was going to slap her.

"I'm yo flesh and blood," he screamed, beating on his chest. "You left me in a orphanage for all of those years. I'm not the smartest person in the world, but I know right from wrong." He wiped the tears with the back of his hand. "You know what, though, I'ma kill you with kindness."

Aunt Roz hugged his neck so tight that he thought that she was about to strangle him. She didn't say it, but Duke knew she was sorry. Her guilt was the reason that she fought for custody of him. This is how "Family first" became the motto.

Chapter 1
Birth of a Dynasty

It takes some people a lifetime to realize that they will never see the good life. For Duke, this was a different story. His mom and dad were hustlers, so a hustler he would also be. Aunt Roz didn't want him in the streets, but Duke chose to hustle anyway. She tried her best to fill the empty void, but she was no match for what the streets had to offer. Living two houses down from a crack house only made it that much worse.

The first time that Duke met Cent, she was coming down the alleyway behind Aunt Roz's house. You couldn't tell by looking at her, but Cent wasn't your average crack smoker. Every time that a car drove up, she was the one who went to get their dope for them. The only people who didn't send her to get their dope were Luv's personal customers.

Luv was Cent's dope supplier and next-door neighbor; Luv had it or lockdown. The only flaw that Duke saw in the operation was Luv's attitude: he treated Cent like shit, and she was making him big bucks, hand or fist. Instead of voicing an opinion, Duke bought a double up and went on the block. The only problem was he didn't know how to hustle.

Duke gave away more dope than what he sold. Crackheads were fighting over who would buy dope from him. Cent didn't make it no better; she saw his weakness and exploited it every chance that she could.

A car drove up to Cent's house, and Duke served them something for fifty. Before the car was out of the driveway, Cent's brother, Ram, came running down the stairs.

"Why you hit my lick."

"You tripping, I been serving them people all morning," Duke told him while sticking the money in his pocket.

He poked Duke in the chest. "Shortstop one more of my licks and I'ma beat yo ass."

"You got me fucked."

Ram had his hands wrapped around Duke's throat before he could finish. It took a few minutes, but he slipped out of the death grip and gave Ram a two-piece to the head. Ram swung, missed, and slipped down in the muddy driveway. Duke took advantage of his mishaps and proceeded to stomp a mud hole in Ram. Cent's son, Zebo, ran up from behind and pulled Duke off of his uncle.

"Nigga, don't grab me," Duke spat out, jerking away from him.

"I'm just tryna break it up."

"I don't give a fuck what you are trying to do. You put yo hands on me again, and me and you gone fight."

Before he could respond, Cent came running downstairs, clutching a glass pipe in her palm.

"Time out," she screamed, raising her hands in the air. "I need to be paid by whomever just hit that lick." She looked back and forth.

Duke gave her a ten-dollar bill and left without another word. He made it home and dumped everything out of his pockets onto the bed. Duke searched through the money and still didn't see his dope.

"Fuck," he spat out, sitting on the bed counting the crumpled-up dollar bills.

It was after 2:00 a.m. and someone was knocking at his bedroom door. He flipped the blanket over, the money, and laid on it.

"Come in."

He knew Aunt Roz was about to start tripping when the door swung open.

"You selling dope?" she asked, leaning against the doorframe.

It didn't take a rocket scientist to notice the new Airmax and Jordans that he wore every day. How else could he afford them? Aunt Roz knew that she hadn't bought them. Although he knew that she knew, he wasn't about to tell on himself.

"Nah, I ane selling no dope. Who told you some mess like that?" he replied, trying to sound as innocent as possible.

"Duke, I know you selling dope. You might as well keep it real with me, and I can take you off my lease." She shifted from one leg to the other "I can't have Section 8 kicking me out because Jackboyz or the jumpout boys running up in here."

"I told you . . . I'm not hustling," he screamed and walk past her.

As soon as he walked up, a truck pulled into Cent's driveway.

"What up?" he asked, getting in the truck.

"Give me something for $500," the driver responded.

Duke didn't have a crumb of dope, but he had a pistol in his pants.

"Where the money?"

"Where the dope?"

They went back and forth for a few minutes before the driver said, "Let's ride around the block."

He turned the ignition switch, and Duke grabbed the clutch, knocking the truck out of gear. He reached for the keys, and the two white boys started tussling with him. The driver finally got the truck started and pulled out of the driveway. By now, Duke was too scared to try to pull the pistol. He figured they would probably wrestle it from him, and maybe even kill him. Duke reached out to open the door and was pushed out. He hit the ground, rolled over, and rose up, shooting. His legs and arms were burning—plus, he had lost one of his new Airmax. First, he lost his dope, and now this. Today wasn't his day.

Duke woke up the next morning sore and aching from head toe. He didn't know that Aunt Roz was in his room until she sat on his bed.

"You ain't finna be staying up all night and sleeping all day in my house . . . Get up," she told him, snatching the covers off him.

"Stop." He pulled the cover back over his head. "Go cook something or something."

"Nigga, who I look like . . . Better call one of your little chicken heads."

Duke rolled over and looked in her face when she said that. This was the first time that Aunt Roz had come at him like that. Aunt Roz really wasn't his aunt; she was adopted and grew up in the same house as Big Duke. As of lately, he was starting to notice the little sly things that she was doing around the house. Like walking around half naked and getting dressed with her bedroom door wide open. It was hard not to look because her 36-24-44 measurements were unbelievable. Duke couldn't tell what was going on inside of her head, but he knew that she was making her ass shake extra hard as she left out of his room.

He peeped out through the blinds for the third time and realized that he wasn't tripping. Police cars were everywhere. Thirty minutes later, once the coast was clear, he slipped out of the back door. Cent saw him coming.

"Some crazy muthafucka tried to rob Trippy and shot him."

"You lying," he shot back, sounding surprised.

"Yep . . . now give me a hit so I can start my day off."

"You know that I don't keep no dope at Aunt Roz crib."

Cent gave him an "I know you lying" look, but she didn't press the issue. "Just bring me something back, once you go get it."

"All right."

Duke saw his cousin Shagg pulling up to Aunt Roz's house just as he was walking out of Cent's house. From past experience, he knew that his cousin was up to no good. That was the only time that he came around.

"I got a lick," he said as soon as Duke was in earshot.

"What type of lick you got this time?"

He pointed over at the truck that he had just got out of. "Me and my boy just came from over this white boy crib. The nigga got a gang of weed and money in that bitch."

"An you think we can pull it off?"

"Well—"

He snatched the blunt out of Shagg's hand. "Hold up, let me get this shit straight. You want me to go where with you and rob who?"

"I promise you that it is as easy lick, cuzz. Ain't nobody in there but the white boy and his girlfriend."

Duke didn't know why but he was letting Shagg drag him into another one of his grand schemes. Before they even made it to the house, Duke knew that something was wrong. His gut instincts told him that he was walking into a trap. Yet after smoking three sticks of PCP, he felt like Superman. The voices in his head grew louder and louder as he got closer to the door. He watched a minivan ride by and opened the screen door.

"Put cha fucking hands on yo head and drop down to yo knees," he demanded, walking into the house.

Duke thought that he was tripping because it seemed as if time had stopped. No one was moving or saying a word. He picked the white boy off who fit the description that he had been given.

"You"—Duke grabbed him by the back of his neck—"give me what I came for, and I won't hurt nobody."

"What, I don't got nothing."

Duke hit him with the gun, and blood shot out of his nose. The other five people standing around looked like they were about to attack him, but Duke waved the gun in their direction.

"Get the fuck back."

He sat Joe in the middle of the small hallway and stood facing the kitchen, where everyone else was now on their knees. To his right and left, there were bedrooms. The door was open, and the light was on his left, but it was the complete opposite on his right. Joe's mom heard the commotion outside of her bedroom door and stuck her head out of the door on the right. She saw Duke with the gun to Joe's head and tried to slam the door back. Duke saw movement out of the corner of his eye and spun around. He kicked the door as hard as he could, sending her flying to the floor with a hard thud.

"Get up and get in the kitchen, you too," he demanded the man lying across the bed. "If you reach for anything, I'ma put a hole in yo fucking head. Now get the fuck in the kitchen."

He marched Mom and Dad into the kitchen, butt-ass naked, to join everyone else on their knees. Duke was beyond frustrated. He only had three bullets in the gun, but he had eight people to shoot if things went bad.

"This my last time asking you where the shit at . . . Stand up." He snatched Joe up by the back of his shirt. "What's in yo pockets?"

Duke found four rubber-banded stacks of money in his socks. He scanned the faces of the three women on their knees and took a lucky guess.

"Go get the weed, or I'ma kill you and him."

She stood there looking at him as if Duke was playing. Duke hit Joe in the ear with the gun and pulled the trigger at the same time. Joe screamed so loud that he had to hit him in the mouth to shut him up.

"Now go get the weed, or I'ma put a bullet in you." She ran into the room on the left and rummaged through a pile of trash bags. Duke got crunk because he knew he was about to get what he had come for.

"Bring it all, or I'ma put a bullet in everybody, in this bitch." She came out of the room with a hefty black trash bag and tossed it into the living room.

"Here . . . take what you came for and leave us alone," she screamed, with tears rolling down her cheeks.

Duke saw the weed falling out of the bag and ran into the living room. As soon as he turned his back, Duke heard a stampede behind him.

"Get back . . . get back . . . get back, bitch. Get back," he spat out while waving the gun from side to side.

He twisted the doorknob with his back against the door and ran as fast as he could. They gave chase, but it was useless. Duke made it four houses down, and Shagg bent the corner in front of him. He leaped onto the back of the truck, and they fled the scene. As soon as they made it back to Aunt Roz's house, Duke stashed the money and half of the weed before splitting anything with them.

"Why the fuck you send me in there with a .25 automatic," he asked, tossing Shagg the gun. "It was eight people in that bitch, and you know I ain't have nothing but three bullets."

"Cuzz—"

"Don't trip, here." He tossed Shagg a block of weed. "Let the white boy leave and you chill wit me for the night."

"Nah, cuzz, I got some shit to take care of."

Duke watched Shagg walk out of the door, and it would be a couple years before they would see each other again. Shagg went to jail that same night and was charged with strong arm robbery. He pled to a lesser charge and was sentenced to seven and a half years as a first offender.

*   *   *   *

Chapter 2
Love, Live, Learn

When he came home and found that his room had been ransacked, Duke knew that his money, dope, and weed were gone.

"Fuck," he said, kicking one of the empty shoeboxes.

He snatched the bottom drawer out on the dresser; the three ounces of crack and fifteen ounces of powder were gone.

"Duke," someone called out from the bathroom.

"No . . . stop," he shouted, rushing into the bathroom.

"Get off me," she spat out, pushing him away. "You said you wasn't hustling."

She flushed the three ounces of crack down the drain before he could catch them. Duke saw the ounces of powder sitting on the sink. Aunt Roz saw him looking at it, and she grabbed the Ziploc bag.

"I don't like what you doing, but I'ma support you because I love you. It's about time that you learn how to make some real money."

"Why you flushing my dope down the tolit, if you wanna see me make some real money."

"Because you lied to me."

She tossed him a Ziploc bag with his money in it and waved her hand to him to follow her into the kitchen. She took out a box of baking soda, some Pyrex jars, and a blender.

"Do you know what this is for?"

"No," he answered, really not knowing.

"You mean to tell me that you got all of that powder and you don't know how to cook it."

"I let Cent cook it for me."

Aunt Roz laughed so hard that her eyes start to water up. "How you gone trust a crackhead to cook yo dope. It's no wonder why they say the smoker love you." The smile on her face faded as fast as it had come. "Don't ever trust a muthafucka with something that you don't know nothing about."

Duke wanted to say fuck it and let her keep the dope after she read him the way that she did. He stood up to leave but was pushed back down into the chair.

"I'ma divide these 15 ounces up into twenty grams apiece, that's 21 ounces. I'ma whip them up with that." She pointed to the stuff sitting on the counter. "When I finish, all of these ounces gonna weigh 28 grams or betta, hustler."

He shook his head. "I don't believe you can do it, and if you do, them ounces ain't gone be worth shit."

"See, that's why the game is so fucked up right now. You niggaz young with all the smarts and no common sense. I never said that it would be the best dope in the world. I'm only saying that they are gonna smoke it."

Before he could argue with her, she grabbed Duke by the arm.

"Watch and listen, because I'm only gonna do this once."

She put 20 grams of coke, a teaspoon of baking soda, and some water in one of the Pyrex jars.

"This gone transform the powder into its gel form. You put a saucer over the top, like this one." She held up a white-and-blue saucer. "The saucer is to keep the fumes under control. Put the Pyrex jar in the microwave, and it should take two to three minutes. The better the dope is, the faster that it will come back."

The powder began to dissolve as they stood in front of the microwave, leaving brown gel on the bottom of the Pyrex jar. Aunt Roz took the jar out and dabbed cold water over the rim.

"Don't ever run water into the jar. Do just as I'm doing. Now it's time for the real magic. You have to pour some of the water out, but make sure to keep enough so that it will be able to hold the baking soda you plan to use. This is what you call whipping work.

Duke felt like a sponge, absorbing everything that she did and said. Aunt Roz put two teaspoons of baking soda in the glass, and then she used the blender to whip the dope like cake batter. The blender turned around and around until she finally sat the jar on the counter.

"You gone know when it's time to stop whipping it, because you gone feel it start to get hard. If you don't stop whipping, you gone fuck it up, but you can always recook it and try again."

Duke saw her lips moving, but he couldn't hear a word that she said. His attention was on the cookie inside of the Pyrex jar. Aunt Roz drained the water off the cookie and sat it on the saucer.

"Why it came out so thick? The cookies that I get from Cent always be thin."

"That's because she stealing all of your dope." She grabbed the digital scale out of the cabinet and dropped the cookie on. "Look at that, 32 grams."

She let him see it with his own eyes before continuing, "Duke, you gotta quit thinking so dam small. You don't have to stand on a corner and hustle no mo. Put the word out that you got ounces for 750 and niggas gone start looking for you. I'm talking about the niggaz that you think balling." She lit a Newport, took a long drag, and blew the smoke in his face. "Always remember that a fool can make money, but it takes a smart nigga to do something with the money. Now finish cooking up this shit and go get paid."

She turned to walk away, and his eyes zeroed in on her ass.

"Oh yea"—she looked back over her shoulder—"quit looking up my ass."

Selling weight made it hard for Duke to keep dope. He decided to go to the projects to find a new supplier because his connect got busted on the interstate. Duke walked from building to building, leaving empty-handed every time. Frustrated and mad at the world, Duke sat on the hood of the rental truck, smoking a blunt.

"What's yo name, youngsta?"

"You ain't gotta make small talk, homie. Just ask to hit the blunt," he said, passing the blunt.

Biggs took the blunt and sat on the hood beside him.

"You gone tell me yo name."

"Duke."

"Well, peep this here, Duke. I been watching you, and I wanna put you on my team." He held out his hand. "How much money you got?"

"A few dollars," he replied and slid off the truck.

Bigg took a Ziploc bag out of his hood sweater and held it out to Duke.

"I'ma put you on yo feet, li'l nigga. This what yo daddy did for me when I was yo age."

"How much I owe you?" Duke asked, looking at the cookies.

"I'ma give you all 18 for eight grand."

Duke pulled out a stack of money. "That's six grand, I'a bring you the rest in the morning."

"OK, holla at me," he replied and walked away.

From that day forward, Duke and Biggs were thick as thieves. Word got around that he was putting Duke on and the hating began. Biggs girlfriend Precious was cool with him, but her best friend, Shamekia, couldn't stand Duke. Every time they saw one another, they were at each other's throat. Shamekia and

Biggs's cousin were an off-and-on couple. Zae couldn't stand Duke because he was jealous that Biggs was showing him love. Then he felt like Shamekia and Duke had something going on. Although they didn't, Duke still rubbed it in his face every chance that he got. One day they were playing the PlayStation, and Biggs hollered, "Lil' nigga, I'ma make you rich."

Surprised was an understatement. Duke didn't know what to say after Biggs told him that. He didn't want to say anything to make him change his mind. Duke just nodded his head.

*   *   *   *   *

Chapter 3
Burn Ya Block Down and Give It Back

Cent was a real con artist. If a big-time customer came to her house, she turned tricks and everything to keep them buying dope. After they spent every dime in their possession, then, and only then, were they allowed to leave. If their girlfriend was with them, she would fuck and suck whoever had dope for sale. Everything was running smooth on Allen Avenue; Duke had the block sowed up. Hustling was now his full-time job, and he put in as many hours as possible. In a few weeks, he was rock for rocking almost a whole bird. The money was coming in so fast that licks were lined up bumper to bumper, ten cars at a time.

Shagg was granted parole and came home early. Duke put him on his feet as soon as he touched down. He took Shagg shopping, gave him money, dope, and some customers to sell the dope to. The game was so good that Duke now had people hustling for him. Traffic, traffic, traffic. Duke turned Allen Avenue into a million-dollar spot; the licks never stopped coming. He spent so much time at Cent's house that you would think that he lived there. The garage was fixed up like a one-bedroom apartment. Big-screen TV, king-sized bed, two couches, a PlayStation, and a refrigerator. Duke sold dope, shot dice, and fucked all day. Before long, almost half of the south side were getting their dope from him, one way or the other. On Friday nights, Duke made so much money that he had to go re-up every ten minutes.

Duke was also starting to spend a lot of time in Parkview with Shamekia. He'd sit over at her mom's apartment all night getting high. As soon as they went over to Precious's apartment, their attitudes changed. Shamekia was twenty-one, and Duke was sixteen; but she admired how mature he was. Not to mention that he was hood rich. Duke tried to take her to Aunt Roz's house one night, and she laughed at him. When he tried to take her to a motel, she told him no. It took a month before they finally had sex. Duke was between her legs, pushing and putting his back into it, but Shamekia did seem to be enjoying herself.

"Take the rubber off."

"Why?" he asked, looking dumbfounded.

"Take it off so that I can feel it, or get off of me."

He wanted to say no, but he couldn't fix his lips to say it.

"You ain't gonna kill me, huh."

"Boy"—she start laughing—"you is too dam crazy."

A week later, he was in the club sitting by the bar, and Hotboy pointed out a female on the dance floor.

"There go yo girl."

He looked up and saw Shamekia bending over, half of her ass hanging out of the dress that she was wearing. She must have seen the look on his face because she followed him out of the club when the music stopped.

"Where you going?" she asked, standing in front of him, one hand on her hip.

"Don't let me stop you from having fun. Gone back in the club and finish shaking yo ass."

Shamekia took off one of her high heels. "Make me break out your dam windows . . . make me. You better take me home before I start clowning."

Duke wasn't the least bit scared, but he knew that she was serious by the look on her face. Duke didn't want to cause a big scene in front of everyone. He spent the night with Shamekia and moved in with her the following day.

Although he was now living in Parkview, Duke still woke up early every morning to go hustle on Allen Avenue. Shamekia was his girl, but he still slept with La La every chance that he got. She was one female that he knew would stick around through thick and thin. La-La could see him with another woman and not even trip. If there was a jealous bone in her body, she never let it show. La-La was labeled a whore around the hood, but it was hard to tell. She stood five feet seven, had a caramel complexion, long wavy hair, and the body of a model. Duke didn't care what they said about her; she was his whore.

One Friday night, he was pulling an all-nighter on Allen Avenue. Aunt Roz was out of town for the weekend, and Shamekia was at the club. La-La kept calling his phone, but he didn't answer because he was with another female. Duke and India were naked at Aunt Roz's house. India was facedown, Duke was pounding her out from behind, and someone started knocking at his bedroom window. Duke was so caught up in the moment that he got up to answer the door. He opened the door, saw La-La standing there, and slammed the door in her face.

"Get up, get up," he told India when he ran back into the room. "Put yo dam clothes on."

He took India in the kitchen and unlocked the side door.

"I want you to go out of this door when you hear me talking at the front door."

La-La was still standing at the door when he opened it.

"Why you slam the door in my face?" she asked with her arms folded across her chest.

"I don't know."

"Where the bitch at, then?"

"Girl, ain't nobody in here."

She pushed past him and went straight to his bedroom. LaLa lifted the blanket over her head and shook it. India's bra and panties hit the floor.

"Who that's for?" she asked, looking upside his head "I don't wear that type of shit."

Before he could come up with a good lie, the dogs in the backyard started barking. She ran past Duke and out the door. La-La came back five minutes later with tears in her eyes and the face of a mad black woman.

"I started to beat that hoe up but my beef is with you. I told her to go wash yo dick off her breath and come back."

"Yo ass crazy."

"Nah, I wanna see if you fuck her like you fuck me. So I'm praying that she comes back."

The money and all of the women had Luv hating on Duke. He didn't know it but that was who told La-La he was with India. Whenever they were with one another, it was all love; but behind his back, Luv called him everything but a child of God. Duke was sitting in Aunt Roz's yard talking on his cell phone when Pam came strolling down the street. Her and Shagg were creeping together on the lowdown, but she also had a fetish for women. Duke was about to speak, but she never gave him a chance to.

"I'm not trying to be messy or nothing, but that nigga Luv is a hater."

"Why you say that?"

"We was getting high night before last, and he start tripping. Luv said Biggs fronting you kilos and what not, but if it wasn't for him, you wouldn't be shit."

Duke gave her words time to sink in before responding. This wasn't the first time that he had heard something like that.

"I'ma call that bitch-ass nigga. When he get here, I want you to repeat what you just said to me."

"Call him over here, and I'ma tell him exactly what I just said." Luv wasn't living on Allen anymore, but he hadn't moved far away. For the past six months, Duke had been fronting him dope, so he was really pissed off. Ten minutes later, Luv drove up, and Pam repeated exactly what she had said that he said.

"You lying bitch," he spat out and punched Pam in the mouth.

Duke step between them "why you so mad if she lying, then."

"Duke, you know that me and you are better than that. That bitch."

Duke hit him in the mouth and didn't quit swinging. Aunt Roz heard something bumping up against the house and came outside. She squeezed in between them and pried Duke's hands from around Luv's neck.

"You making my fucking house hot . . . I told you about this shit."

"You a hoe," Luv told him, wiping the blood from his nose onto his shirt.

"Me and you can catch the street if you feeling played. I'm through with all of that talking, playboy."

"You gone get cha issue, you ca—"

Duke spat in his face. "You can hide behind Aunt Roz all you want, but I'm catch you in the streets."

Aunt Roz pulled a gun out of her apron pocket and shot twice in the air.

"I want everybody out my muthafucking yard and off my street befo' I start busing heads. You muthafuckas is losing y'all minds. I don't know where you think y'all at, and who the fuck you think you are?"

Duke saw the look on her face and knew that she meant every word. He wanted to argue with her but didn't want to say something that he would regret later. Luv's four-door Cutlass sparkled as he drove away. Looking at the peanut butter ragtop, interior, center gold rims and hearing like 4 twelves in the trunk made Duke even madder. He drove a '77 Catalina, and it didn't look nothing like Luv's car, but Duke wasn't worried about it. He was more concerned about adding to his stash.

"Hello."

"I need a favor."

"You know it's whatever with me," Hustleman said with a smile plastered on his face.

"I want you to burn that nigga Luc's car up. I don't care if it is inside of a garage—torch the house and all if you have to."

"Enough said. You already know that I never liked that nigga anyway."

Duke took a shower and lay down for some much-needed rest. It seemed as if as soon as he closed his eyes, Shamekia shook him awake.

"What . . . dam." He groaned, rolling over.

"This shit is driving me crazy." She handed him all three of his cell phones. "Get up and answer these fucking hotlines."

Duke, grab the phones from her and answered one of them. "Hello," he shouted in a grouchy voice.

"I don't know what's going on, but you need to get over here ASAP. Luv done told the detectives and the fire marshal that you burned up his car."

Tension was definitely in the air as Shamekia drove down dick. Taylor Street on her way to Aunt Roz's house. Crowds of people were standing around waiting for a fight or some gunplay to jump off.

Luv and a group of people were standing in front of his house as Shamekia drove by. Duke let the window down, chunked up the deuce, and turned the beat back up. Aunt Roz ran over to his car as soon as it pulled in the driveway.

"What happen?" he asked, getting out of the car.

"I came outside and saw a ball of fire down the street. At first I didn't know what the fuck was happening." She snatched the blunt out of Duke's hand. "I hope you ain't have shit to do with that because his baby mama almost got killed. She was in the house sleep when the gas tank exploded."

"I been at home sleep," he responded with a smirk on his face.

"Boy, you know what the hell I mean."

Duke looked down at the iPhone vibrating on his hip. "I gotta go, call me if you need something."

"Duke, don't go do nothing crazy. You know I know you better then you know yourself."

Allen Avenue went from being under the radar to the hottest street around the city. The police started riding up and down Allen all day and night. Some nights they would sit on the corner across from Aunt Roz's house and pull over ever call that left out of her driveway. One night Duke, Shagg, Will, and Hotboy were getting ready for the club. Shagg's phone rang, and he had to make a run.

"You want me to take you?" Duke asked, wondering where he was going.

Although, he knew that if Shagg had a lick he wasn't going to take him. He gave smokers three rocks for twenty.

"Nah, it's just right around the corner. I'a be back in about five minutes."

Duke, Will, and Hotboy sat around getting high waiting on Shagg to come back. The dogs in the front yard started barking, and Duke thought that it was Shagg. He opened the front door and regretted that he did. Mickey was the last person that he wanted to see, but he tried not to show it.

"Hey sexy," he said with a smile.

She handed him three shopping bags. "They didn't have blue T-shirts."

Mickey was a good girl, pretty in the face, and had long, wavy hair. She was just a little too thick for his taste. Mickey did everything that he asked her to do, and he hadn't even slept with her. She followed him to his bedroom and sat down beside him on the bed.

"I can't chill long because I'm clubbing tonight," he told her, lying back on the bed.

"What I got to say ain't gonna take long." She looked in his eyes. "We been knowing one another for over a year, and we still havn't."

Duke unzipped his pants and put his hand on the back of her neck. "Make me feel good, and we can talk about this a little later."

Mickey let her head drop to his lap like she had been trained to do. Suck, lick, slurp, and swallow every drop before raising her head back up. The puppy look on her face made Duke give in. He bent her over on the bed and hit Mickey from behind. Her pussy was so hot and wet that Duke surprised himself. He stroked her for fifteen minutes. When they finished, Mickey went in her purse, pulled out an envelope, and dropped it on the bed on her way out of the door. Duke counted the money before putting it in his safe. Pimping wasn't easy, nor fair, but it damn sure paid good. He took out another one of the pressed-up outfits from his closet and took a quick shower. When he walked back into the living room, they fell over laughing.

"Dam, we thought she smothered yo ass," Hotboy said, falling back on the couch.

"Shut up, that shit ain't funny. Where the fuck is that nigga Shagg at. See, this why . . . who is it," he asked, looking through the peephole.

"Me."

Duke opened the door, and his mouth dropped to the floor, right along with everyone else's.

"What the fuck happen to you?"

"Man, I met up with my white boy on South Grand. I walked up to the car and stuck my hand in the window. He grabbed my arm and put the car in reverse. That bitch drug me for almost a block," Shagg explained, looking and sounding pitiful.

Duke shook his head, not really knowing what to say. "Go get you some alcohol, peroxide, or whatever it is that you gone need." He looked down at the Rolex on his wrist. "You need to be ready for the club in the next twenty minutes."

Spicy beef was cooking on Allen. Luv bought some guns and grew King Kong balls overnight. Shamekia was driving down Lee Avenue, and Luv shot at Duke's car. She hit the curb and bent two of his rims trying to get away. Duke knew something was wrong as soon as Shamekia came speeding down Allen. She pulled into the driveway, and he saw that the back driver's side looked like Swiss cheese.

"What happened?"

"They . . . they . . . they was shooting at me," she responded while still holding on to the steering wheel with both hands.

Duke ran into the house and came back with a Mac-11 with a towel wrapped around it.

"Take me back around there."

"I don't—"

"Well, get the fuck out of the car."

She took him to Cent's house, but everybody was gone. Shamekia drove him over to Luv's house, and he hopped out before the car came to a complete stop. He let off fifteen shots at the house and stood there. He realized that no one was crazy enough to come outside and emptied the rest of the 30-round clip on the two cars sitting in the driveway. Cent came running through the alleyway as soon as Shamekia pulled back into Aunt Roz's driveway.

"You wrong, Duke, and you know it. Let's let this bullshit go and keep getting to the money. It's enough money out here for everybody."

Duke shook his head. "I don't care what you say, Cent. I'ma bat his ass up when I catch him."

Cent saw that he wasn't in a good mood and left. Duke cranked up the Friday night dice game as soon as the sun went down. Carloads of gamblers were pulling up and pulling off. Two unmarked police cars hit the block with their lights off and drove upon the grass. Duke was the first person to take off running. He left a bag of rocks and his cell phone wrapped up in a Pelle Pelle shirt. The officers were searching so hard that they looked right over the Mac-11 and a quarter pound of hydro. Duke had it stashed in an old speaker box over by the tree. One of the officers picked the Pelle-Pelle shirt up, and everything hit the ground. He grabbed the rocks and went looking for Duke. Shagg, Hotboy, Will, and Pam were released. The police let everybody else go too because they said they knew who it belonged to. The head hunce of Metro Narcotics came to the scene to have a talk with Aunt Roz.

"Do you know about the criminal activities taking place in your backyard?"

"Criminal activities?"

"Yes, we found over 400 rocks of crack cocaine in your backyard."

Rose put a hand on her hip. "Look, I work a twelve-hour shift every day and come home to rest the other twelve. I don't have time to patrol what goes on in my yard because that's your job. I advise you to start doing it."

Aunt Roz found Duke hiding in the attic after the police left.

"I told you about this shit, but you so fucking hardheaded. This my last time telling yo ass, though. If I catch anybody hustling in my yard, you going to jail, do you hear me?" she asked, poking him in the chest.

Allen Avenue was good while it lasted, but everything was all bad now. Duke packed up the rest of his things and left without even saying good-bye. It was time to start over fresh, and Parkview was the best place for that.

* * * *

Chapter 4
Straight Out of Parkview

Parkview was definitely more different than Duke could remember. It was all love, but it was far from being Allen Avenue. The first day he was in Parkview, it turned out to be pure hell. Some dude smoked too many sticks of PCP and stripped down butt naked in the parking lot. Duke and Biggs sat around laughing as they watched him chase a woman around the building with a bottle in his hand. Things really got out of hand when the cable guy drove up.

"What chu doing?" he asked, running up to the cable man.

The cable man pissed his pants staring at the naked man standing in front of him.

"I-I-I'm disconnecting."

He grabbed the cable man, snatched the clipboard, and pushed him to the ground.

"You ain't finna do shit."

The cable man jumped up and ran back to his truck. "I'm just doing my job."

"Leave my people alone . . . leave my people alone!" he screamed, climbing on top of the truck, kicking the windshield.

Five minutes later, the police drove up, and things got even worse.

"Get down and put your hands on your head," they demanded, drawing their guns.

He didn't comply, and they applied extensive force. One of the officers grabbed hold of one of his legs and snatched him clean off of the truck. He knocked the officer down, and the other three officers Maced him down. Four more cars drove up, and they put Rodney King's beating to shame. The officers beat, pepper-sprayed, and dragged the naked man for thirty minutes. Duke sat back and watched the who escapade take place, knowing a hot, long, and crazy summer was on its way.

"I got that sixty grand that I owe you, and I'ma need some more work tomorrow," he told Biggs.

Biggs smiled. "I told you that it's some money out here."

"It's cool, but I'm not making the type of profit that I was making on Allen."

"Quit thinking so fucking small all the time. It's a lot of money out here, and you either want it or you don't."

Duke wasn't making the type of profit that he was used to making, but it was coming faster than he could count it. Biggs left when he saw how much traffic was coming to Shamekia's apartment. It was too much for him in so many ways. Hustling in Parkview was a dream come true. There was so much money to be made that you couldn't go wrong if you were selling weight. The biggest hustle in Parkview was to outhustle the hustlers. You have slick people all over the world, but Parkview people are a different story. If you give someone less than their money's worth, they're happy as can be. They only feel cheated when you do give them their money's worth. A drought hit Parkview, and Duke was sitting on birds. The constant flow of traffic was making him paranoid. He had never seen anything like it in his life. So much traffic was in and out of Shamekia's apartment that he stayed up for a week straight. He tried to make people call before stopping by, but that didn't work. In four days, he made about a quarter of a million, and only eighty-five thousand of that belonged to Biggs. The money started coming in so fast that he didn't get to spend it.

Duke was making money in Parkview, but that didn't guarantee him respect. He caught young Rome shortstopping his licks and pulled him to the side.

"I don't got no problem with you getting money, homie. I just can't have you harassing the people who coming to holler at me."

He looked at Duke sideways. "Yea, whatever," he said before walking away.

Two days later, he caught young Rome doing the same thing. Duke wasn't as nice this time. He put young Rome in a chokehold and took everything out of his pockets, including the gun in his waistband. Later that night, someone was kicking on the door of Shamekia's apartment. Duke paused the game, and Hotboy got up to answer the door.

"Who is it?"

"Big Body, Duke in there?"

Duke grabbed the gun off the table and stuck it in his pants before going outside.

"What's up?" Duke asked, walking out of the door.

"Rome said you took—"

"Hold up—" He raised his hand. "I ain't take shit from that bitch-ass nigga. I told him to quit fucking wit my people, and he ain't listen, he gave me that."

"Well, I'm here to get that back, then. That was my shit that you took."

"That's between you and him."

"I should smack the shit out of you."

Shagg and Hotboy appeared out of thin air and leaned against the wall.

Duke laughed. "You must don't know who the fuck I am."

Big Body reached out to grab Duke, and a gun went off. It happened so fast that Duke thought that he had been shot. Big Body tumbled down the stairs, got up to run, and fell dead on the sidewalk.

"Why you shoot him?" Duke asked, looking at Hotboy.

"My gun in the house."

Shagg hunched his shoulders. "Bitch-ass nigga interrupted my sleep. He should be shot."

Duke gathered up his money, dope, and the guns in the apartment. He had some smokers clean the blood up and drag Big Body farther down the sidewalk.

"Where you going?"

"I gotta make a run."

Shamekia looked in his eyes. "What hoe done called you."

Duke and Shamekia's relationship was an emotional roller coaster. One minute they were as happy as can be, and the next minute they were at each other's throat. Shamekia's pussy was the first to have him put his tongue, and you could tell. She loved to tease him and play games because she knew that he was sprung. Every time he tried to be nice, she took him for granted.

"Move." He pushed past her. "You so fucking jealous."

Shamekia snatched the scale and CD cases out of his hand.

"Now, where you said you were going?"

"Gimmie my shit and quit playing all the dam time."

She drew back and threw everything thing down the hallway. The digital scale was the first thing to hit the floor and splatter into a million pieces. Duke slapped Shamekia and, she stumbled back, holding her face.

"You . . . I can't believe you hit me."

"I don't know why I'm wasting my time fucking with your fucking stupid ass."

"Well, leave then, nigga."

Duke met Biggs on the way down the stairs.

"She broke yo scale," he told Biggs, walking toward the parking lot.

"Go buy me another one, then."

"From where? I don't know where to get scales from."

He unlocked the passenger door so Duke could get in. "Holla at dude in the mall that we get the jewelry from."

"How much the cost?"

"Hunit-fifty."

Duke dug in his pocket for the money. "Here go two-hunit."

"Nah, yo gurl broke it, and you gone go get me a new one." Duke was really mad now. He missed a five-thousand-dollar lick because he had to go get Biggs a new scale. The funny thing was that he didn't own a scale of his own.

"My people out, and I'ma have to go find us something. I don't know how long. I'ma be gone, but it shouldn't take no more than a week."

Duke got out the car and slammed the door. "You ain't got shit stashed."

"Two weeks at the most," he told Duke and drove off.

The problems with Shamekia made him hustle like no tomorrow. He was selling weed, crack, powder, PCP, and all kinds of pills. Everything was going good until he ran out of dope. Duke was beginning to feel like the game wasn't meant for him. Biggs was gone and wouldn't return phone calls. Just when he was about to give up, Duke met an ole skool by the name of Polo.

"What up, young blood."

"Shid, you already know me," Duke said, shaking his hand.

"You ready to let me get that regal. You sho do got her looking good on them bullet tips."

"As bad as I'm doing, you can have that piece of shit."

"What, yean grinding no mo," he asked, leaning back against his navigator.

"You already know how it is when it gets dry. I'a do without befo I let a nigga bird feed me."

"Whatcha talking?"

"Two and a half."

"Give me forty grand, and I ca have it on yo doorstep in twenty minutes."

Duke pulled out a stack of money with rubber bands wrapped around it and tossed it to Polo.

"That's ten grand, I'ma give you the rest when you make the drop."

"That's why I like you, young blood. You a straight-up hustler."

Ten minutes after Duke picked the dope up, Biggs showed up at Shamekia's apartment. He gave Duke four birds in a foot locker bag, twenty grand apiece.

"I just bought two and a half from Polo. I didn't know when you was coming back."

"You spent money with that nigga . . . how much he charge you?"

"Forty grand," Duke responded.

A moment of silence passed between them before Biggs said, "You want me to keep that until you get through with—"

"You tripping. You and I both know that I'm about dump this shit."

"All right, holla at me later," he told Duke and left without another word.

Later that night, Duke came into the house and took his shoes off.

"Why you sitting in the dark?" he asked flipping on the light.

Shamekia got up out of the plastic chair that she had been sitting in and got right in his face.

"Where you been, and don't tell me that shit about you been out hustling." She reached for his belt. "Let me smell yo dick, nigga. I know you been out there fucking with them nasty-ass hoes."

He swatted her hand away. "I been out taken care of business. And no, you can't smell my dick."

"Oh . . . OK, then. I left yo food in the oven," she told him and walked out of the room.

Duke took a bath and went straight to sleep. At seven the next morning, he was up and ready to go. His cell phones had been ringing since 6:00 a.m. He went downstairs to warm up his car and found the door locked when he came back.

"Dam," he said, running back downstairs.

He fumbled with the keys on his keyring and saw that his house keys were gone. Duke took his time going back upstairs.

"Open the dam door and quit playing, it's cold out here."

The more he knocked, the madder that he got. The knocking soon turned into him kicking on the door. Precious was standing in her building laughing because Shamekia was in the window talking to her. He was falling all over the ground, kicking on the door getting madder and madder. The door was about to cave in when she finally decided to open it.

"Move" he spat out, pushing past her. "I'ma get my shit and get out of your apartment."

"Nigga . . . please, you ain't going no dam where."

Duke turned his back to her and dialed a number on his cell. "Yea, whatever . . . hello."

"What?"

"Shagg, go get the truck and come help me get my shit from over Shamekia's spot."

"What—"

"Just help me get my shit, bye."

She grabbed Duke by the arm. "Baby, you know I was just playing."

"You took my house key and had me looking like a dam fool kicking on that dam door."

"I thought . . . you know, maybe you need to go over to Aunt Roz's house for a couple days."

"You right . . . I'ma get my shit right now."

When Shagg finally did come, they loaded the truck up. His plan was to take everything that he'd paid for, but he realized that she would need it more than he would.

Shamekia realized that he was serious about leaving and tried to stop him. "I'm not letting you leave," she said, blocking the door.

He pushed Shamekia to the side and left out the door. He loaded up both of his cars and then got in his Catalina. Shamekia rolled a blunt when he left and then went over to Precious's apartment.

"I told you about fucking with that young ass boy," she told Shamekia when she walked through the door.

"Shut up."

"He put all that shit in yo house, and now be gone take it all back."

"I should break his car windows out."

Precious opened the closet door. "There, go the bat in there. I got a hunit dollars that you want, do it."

Duke and Shagg were still unloading the truck when Biggs drove up to Aunt Roz's house.

"I tried to stop her."

Duke gave him a puzzled look. "What the fuck is you talking about."

"Shamekia. She broke all of the windows out of your Regal."

Duke and Shagg jumped back in his Catalina and drove straight to Parkview. He wanted to kill Shamekia when he saw what she had done to his Regal. Out of anger, he went up to her apartment and broke everything that he could put his hands on. Someone knocked on the door as soon as he sat down to catch his breath.

"Who the fuck is it?"

"Monroe Police Department."

He felt his knees get weak when he heard that. Money, dope, and guns were still stashed inside the apartment. Duke started to breathe normal again once he opened the door and saw the two uniformed police officers.

"May I help you?"

"Yes, we received a call from this apartment, but no information was given."

"Oh yea, come on downstairs and let me show you what she did to my car."

The officers examined the Regal and wrote up a report. As soon as they put Shamekia's name in the computer, a red flag popped up.

"Sir, she already has a warrant for her arrest. We're going to be in the area, so call us if you see her," the officers stated and got back in their patrol cars.

By now, Duke was pissed to the third degree. The happy haters laughed as he drove out of Parkview in the battered Regal. If his cell phone hadn't rung, he would have driven clean out of town.

"Hello!"

"You though that I was just gone let you play me, huh?"

"Bitch, you going to jail, or I'ma beat yo ass. Either way it goes, I'ma be happy."

Shamekia hung up on him just as Duke drove back through the front gate of Parkview. The police officers went over to the apartment that they said Shamekia was at.

"Don't be sending the fucking police over here," Precious shouted when she opened the door. "You know she ain't over here."

"Fuck that. You probaly was the one who told her to do it."

Duke knew something was wrong by the look on Shagg's face when he got back in the car.

"What?"

He pointed to the radio.

"Dam!" he screamed, slapping the dashboard. "Why the fuck did you let her take the face off of the radio?"

"I'm not getting in yall shit."

Duke jumped back out of the car and ran around to Shamekia's cousin's girlfriend's apartment. He thought about being nice and knocking on the door, but instead, he kicked it as hard as he could.

"If you don't send her out here, I'ma kick yo door down," he told them while looking around the side of the building.

Just as he was about to kick the door again, Shamekia jumped right out of a side window. He ran up behind her and caught Shamekia just as she made it around the building. She was kicking and punching him, but he held her until the police officers drove up. The officers slammed Shamekia down on the ground so hard that Duke felt sorry for her.

"Y'all ain't got to handle her like that," he told them, reaching down to help her up.

"Get back . . . get back, or you are going to jail with her," they advised Duke while drawing their weapons.

"OK," Duke told them while backing up.

Precious ran up, and before she could open her mouth, they had her in handcuffs. Duke just shook his head as he walked away.

*   *   *   *

Chapter 5
Family Affair

Shagg, Pretty, Trina, Will, Hotboy, Shelby, and Duke attended the Ark-La-Miss State Fair. Everyone was feeling sorry for Duke because he was the only one who didn't have a girlfriend. When it was time to ride the love boats, he was left out. Duke saw a female standing in line by herself and boldly grabbed hold of her arm.

"Ride with me."

"She ain't with you?" she asked, pointing at the 300-pound woman in front of him.

"You got jokes, huh."

From 1 to 10 Duke would give this female an 8. She wasn't ugly, nor was she beautiful; but her body was unexplainable.

"You cold?" Duke asked, seeing that her nipples were rock hard.

She realized what he was looking at and folded her arms across her breasts. "What do you think?"

He took the gray-and-yellow Gucci jacket off and gave it to her. She took it from him and put it on.

"Where yo woman . . . Don't give me that shit about you single. You are too good-looking to not have a woman or two."

"Correction, I had a woman. The question is, where yo man at?"

"To be honest with you, I don't even know."

"Well, I'm a give you my number just in case you don't find him."

She brushed her hair to the side. "I'm not really into dopeboys because they—"

"What makes you think that I'm a dopeboy?"

"Look at you." She looked down at the name on the jacket he gave her. "You got on Gucci from head to toe. A Cartier watch, the bracelet, and sunglasses. That's every bit of twenty-five grand worth of shit. Now, how can you fix yo mouth to say that you not a dopeboy?"

The love boats came to a stop, and she stood up to leave.

Duke grabbed hold of her arm, and she sat back down.

"You can call me whatever you want, baby girl. That's still not going to change the fact that I want you. Now, can I at least get your name?"

"Your eyes were so busy roaming all over my body that I thought you would never ask. I'm Daysha, though."

"All right, Daysha, I'm Duke."

Duke left the state fair with a big smile on his face. He knew that her man wasn't doing something right because she took his number too fast. Over the next couple of weeks, Duke took his time wining and dining Daysha. He took her to the movies, out to eat, the bowling alley, and a couple more places. Duke took her to a motel room a couple of times, but she wouldn't have sex with him. Daysha turned out to be a real piece of work: 5'7", 140 pounds, 36-26-40. She was as thick as a racehorse. Her ass resembled Buffy the Body's in a bathing suit.

One night Duke was in the club alone, sitting around watching a slim female shake her ass in the mirror. He was about to join her, but he looked in the mirror again and saw Daysha standing right behind him.

"Let's dance," she whispered, grabbing his arm.

"I don't dance," he said, looking around to see where she had come from.

She stepped in front of him. "Just move with my ass, then."

He was listening to her, but he wasn't paying her any attention. His focus was on the angry-looking dude who was pushing his way through the crowd.

"You know dude?"

She glanced back over her shoulder and turned right back around. "That's my no-good-ass nigga that you always be asking about."

He walked right up to Daysha, grabbed hold of her arm, and pulled her out of the club. A few hours later, she showed up at Aunt Roz's house crying.

"So what, you crying because he don't want you? It ain't like you look like a monster or some shit." He took her glasses off. "You don't need these, neither.

She wiped the tears from her eyes. "I'ma get in trouble messing with you, I can see it coming."

"What does that mean?"

"It means kiss me and make me feel better."

Duke flipped the lights on and tossed the covers on the floor. Passionate kisses and soft touches led to hot and sweaty sex. He bent Daysha over and fell in love. Duke was mesmerized by the way her ass bounce up and down. He pulled her close to him, using his right hand to finger her clit. All the while, he continued to stroke her and suck on the back of her neck. By the time he realized what he was doing, it was too late. Daysha was squirming as the hot semen shot deep inside of her.

It was raining the next day, but Duke still went to Parkview. He fogged the car up sitting in front of Shamekia's building. Shamekia sat upstairs watching him jump in and out of different cars. She wanted to go downstairs and clown him, but she didn't. Duke sold all of the dope that he had brought with him and bought a bag of weed to leave with. As soon as he drove away from Shamekia's building, his cell phone lit up.

"Talk to me."

"Why you ain't come up here? I know—"

"Hold on." He looked over at Daysha. "You staying the night, or you going home tonight?"

"I gotta work in the morning, baby. Just stop to get me something to eat before you take me home."

He nodded his head and picked the phone back up off of the seat. "Hello?"

"I miss you . . . Come home, please."

Duke wanted to say, *Kiss my ass*, but the words never came out.

"I'a be there tomorrow."

"Why you—"

"I gotta go," he replied before hanging up.

He wanted to explain everything to Daysha but didn't know where to start. How could he tell her that he was still in love with Shamekia but wanted to be with her? As in all men, the dog set in, and he told himself that he could juggle them both. Bright and early the next morning, Duke stopped by the paint shop to pick up the Regal. Shamekia and Precious were sitting in front of Precious's building when he drove up. Duke had one hand out of the window, one hand holding a blunt and his knee controlling the steering wheel. Everyone used to laugh when he drove up in his ragly Catalina. Today, though, those same haters had the dick look.

His food was in the oven, and his favorite kind of Kool-Aid was in the icebox when he made it upstairs. Customers were knocking the door off of the hedge before he could finish putting his clothes away. Duke realized that it was time for him to take his hustle to the next level. He was sitting on five birds of fish scale, and it was a drought. People were paying a thousand dollars an ounce. He cooked 60 ounces or more out of a bird and was making every bit of sixty grand. So much traffic was in and out of Shamekia's apartment that everyone just knew the police were gonna bust in at any moment.

"What?" Duke asked, stopping at the red light.

"I want some KFC."

"Iight," he responded and turned into the drive-thru.

"I don't wanna go through the drive-thru. I wanna go in."

Duke almost banged one of his Daytons on the curb when she said that. He wanted to say no but knew that she would insist on going in anyway. Daysha was supposed to be off today, but she filled in for people sometimes. His prayer was that she was at home today. The cashier had her back to them when they walked through the door. She turned to greet them, and Duke almost ran back out of the door. Her eyes were glued to him, but she didn't say a word.

"Why you staring at my man like that" Shamekia asked Daysha. "You need to get my order together before me and you be fighting up in here."

Daysha was in a state of shock. She gave Duke the "Nigga, you wrong" look and walked away from the counter. Duke's head was hurting so bad when they made it back to the car he couldn't even drive.

"I heard you be fucking her, Duke," she told him before driving off.

"Meaning?" He finished rolling the blunt in his hands.

Shamekia stopped the car in the middle of the street. "I'm not one of them li'l dumb hoes that you be fucking," she spat out, eyeing him up and down.

"I'm not about to argue with you about this dumbass shit. My fucking head is hurting. Drive the dam car."

She was about to press the issue, but his cell phone started ringing.

"What?" he screamed over the music.

"Why . . . why you do me like that? Duke, you wrong, and you know you wrong."

"I'a be that way in thirty minutes."

"Just tell me why you brought her up to my job. Out of all places, why my job?"

"I gotta—"

"Why, Duke, just tell me why. What did I ever do to you to deserve this?"

"I gotta go," he responded and hung up before she could say another word.

Shamekia was staring a hole in the side of his head. "That was yo li'l bitch from KFC, huh?"

"Don't ever question me about who I'm talking to on my fucking phone."

After a year of nonstop traffic, Parkview was hotter than fish grease. The managers over Parkview set up a police base downstairs in Shamekia's building. They thought that that would stop Duke, but it didn't even come close. Between 8:00 a.m. and 5:00 p.m., he met his customers outside of Parkview. Everyone started saying that he was acting funny, but he didn't care because he was on his way to becoming a millionaire. His only downfall was Shamekia. She was always into something. If you tried to tell her anything, you had a fight on your hands. When it came to Duke, she was very possessive. The girl downstairs tried to give him some pussy, and somehow Shamekia found out. Duke was upstairs sleeping when the drama jumped off. They were in the breezeway boxing by the time he came downstairs.

"Don't grab her."

"Break it up, then," someone responded.

Duke blocked the stairwell off when they fell on the stairs so that no one could touch them. The girl pinned Shamekia down, and Duke broke the fight up. Shamekia was calling to the office the next day.

"They evicted me and gave her a warning," she said when she came back.

"You knew that shit would happen, and you out here fighting."

Shamekia started crying. "It's you . . . You selling all this dope out here. You got my fucking apartment hot, and you wanna blame me. You selling dope out here, not me."

Duke knew that this was a no-win situation. He had to reason with her.

"Well, come on, and let's go find us somewhere to stay."

*   *   *   *

Chapter 6
Mo Money, Mo Problems

The more money, the more women, cars, and clothes that come along. Duke was madly in love with Shamekia, but as in every man, he has needs that one woman can't take care of. He met Janell at the Cartier booth in the mall, and they immediately hit it off. Standing four feet nine, she had a body to die for. Duke told her he had a woman, and she was cool with that. He used Janell's house as a safe haven for cooking and stashing his dope. Janell went to work from 7:00 a.m. until 3:00 p.m. and came home expecting Duke to be there.

"I'm tired of you using me for a fuck and place to stash your dope. Why you can't treat me like you treat wifey."

"I'm finna go," he told her as he grabbed the bag from beside the couch.

Duke hated to hear the bitching, but he had to give Janell her props. She was a great cook and didn't mind cleaning or spreading her legs whenever he asked.

"Why you tryna leave, and we havn't even spent any time together, all day."

"I was a hustler when we met, baby girl. You can except that, or go get a new sponsor."

"Oh, that's how you feel now."

Duke grabbed the keys off the countertop. "I'm spending all of this time listening to you talk shit, and I got a woman at home . . . I must be losing my mind."

"If you walk out that door, don't come back."

Duke slammed the door as hard as he could on his way out. Things were going too good to let her sour his mood. He knew that just as fast as it came, it could all be taken away. Therefore he saved every dollar that he wasn't flipping. The only thing he took to heart was the fact that the people that he tried to help were trying to bring him down. Like his cousin Bo, who was holding a safe with seven grand in it. Duke went to empty the safe and couldn't find it. He tore the house up but still didn't find it. Aunt Roz called Bo at his job and found out that he had called in. Duke paged Bo and put 9-1-1 in his pager, over and over again.

"Where the fuck you at?" he screamed, snatching the phone off its base.

"Why you paging me 9-1-1?"

"What, nigga, you better get yo ass over here."

Duke and Aunt Roz were pacing the floor when Bo drove up. Before he could make it in the house, Duke was all over him.

"Where my fucking safe at?"

"It . . . it was upstairs when I left last night."

"Well, we about to go upstairs, and it better be up there."

Everyone went in the house to look around, but the safe was long gone. Bo tried to explain, but Duke wasn't hearing it. He slapped Bo in the face with the pistol and pushed him downstairs. Aunt Rose was about to stop Duke, but the look on his face told her to mind her business. Bo was crying and carrying on, but Duke kept slapping him across the head with the pistol.

"Bitch, shut up," he spat out, slapping him again. "I ain't tryna hear that shit."

The only reason he hadn't shot and killed Bo was that he didn't have the heart to do it. He went over to see Bo's car and used a crowbar to pry the trunk open. He found a gas can and started pouring it all over the car. As he was lighting it, Bo's sister came outside.

"Leave that car alone."

"Shut up, bitch," he shot back, searching his pocket for a lighter.

"I'ma call the police on yo ass . . . Nigga, you ain't nobody."

"You better shut the fuck up befo I shut you up."

She ran into the house to call the police, but Bo grabbed hold of her. Duke set the car on fire and left walking. It wasn't the money he was mad about, because that could always be made up. He was mad because it was the principal of the whole situation. Duke thought Bo would let him know when he needed something, but he was wrong.

*   *   *   *

Biggs, Duke, Shamekia, and her friend Che went to New Orleans for the weekend. It was supposed to be a business trip, but it turned out to be one big party. From clubs to restaurants and anything else they could get themselves into. Duke was tired of the bullshit that Biggs was putting him through, so now, his main interest was finding a new connect.

It hadn't mattered once before, but now he wasn't a dumb young hustler. He had his people make a few calls, but the prices were still sky high, so when finding a new connect didn't materialize, he did some minor shopping and lay around the hotel room. Biggs was trying to fuck Che, but it just wasn't happening. Duke had to rent a room with double beds because she refused to sleep in a room alone with Biggs.

Duke and Shamekia went downstairs to swim and left Biggs alone with Che upstairs. Duke came back upstairs to get some towels and found Biggs laid out across the bed. He figured Che was down the hall getting some ice or something because he didn't see her.

He pushed the bathroom door open and couldn't believe his eyes.

"Ahh," Che screamed, dropping the towel she had been using to dry off with.

She realized that it was Duke standing in the doorway and slowly bent over. He stepped further in the bathroom and closed the door behind him.

"You know Shamekia gone kill you," he joked, staring at the hairy spot between her legs.

"What she don't know won't hurt her, now, will it. I ain't gone tell . . . you gone tell."

He took the towel and bent Che-Che over, spreading her legs. She grab the sides of the commode, and he slid inside her hot womb. He put his left forearm in the small of her back and grab a handful of hair with his right hand.

"Ahh . . . ahh . . . ahhh," she moaned while taking it like a pro.

"You like this, huh," Duke asked tightening the grip on her hair.

Duke kept pounding her as hard as he could, and she seemed to be enjoying it. The bathroom door flew open, and there stood Biggs, mouth hung wide open. Duke looked back over his shoulder and gave him a big smile.

"Shut the door."

Biggs just stood there looking wide-eyed.

"Dam, nigga, shut the dam door."

"Hell, nah . . . the hoe ain't wanna fuck me because she wanted to fuck you all along."

Che opened her mouth to tell Duke to stop, but she was too weak to speak. Duke pulled out of her, letting the cum shoot all over her lower back and the top of her ass. After cleaning himself up, Duke went back downstairs.

"What took you so long?" Shamekia asked, sitting on the edge of the pool with her feet in the water.

"I won some easy money from Biggs on the game."

"Well, we must be gone. Split it because you done had me waiting on you for about twenty minutes."

After a quick swim, they went back upstairs to shower. Biggs was sitting on the bed, and Che was nowhere to be found.

"Where Che?" Shamekia asked Biggs.

"Outside in the car."

As soon as Shamekia left the room, Biggs began to try to pry it out of Duke.

"How was it?"

"It was cool," he responded, busting a cigar over the trash can.

"It was cool . . . that's it."

Truth be told, it was better than good but Duke didn't feel like going into details.

"What more can I say, it was cool."

*   *   *   *

Duke woke up Sunday morning to a lick for a half of a key. Before he could wash his face or brush his teeth, Duke was off to the projects. It was rolling so hard out there that he decided to stay for a few more hours.

"Hello," the sleepy voice answered.

"I need you to bring me my lovie knapsack, right now."

Biggs and Duke stood in Precious's building smoking on a blunt waiting on Shamekia to pull up. Customer after customer drove up in front of the building, and Duke's cell phone was ringing nonstop. Shamekia bought him a key and a half; it was gone before they could finish the second blunt.

"You making a killing, huh," Biggs said with a smile.

"Nah, I'm just getting started."

On the way back home, his stomach was turning flips. He unlocked the front door, and a strong wind hit him in the face.

Duke pushed the door open and knew something wasn't right. His heart stopped beating when he stepped foot in his bedroom. All his clothes and a thousand other things were lying on the bed. The dresser his safe was built in was broken up into a million pieces and scattered all over the room.

"My safe," he said in total disbelief.

Duke ran into the kitchen and found the back door leaning up against the icebox.

"Hello? Somebody just broke in my crib and stole my shit."

"What!" Biggs responded with a smile.

"Please tell me that you on."

"I got something for you, but it's gone cost."

Duke took the mirror off the bathroom wall and opened his backup safe. "I ain't tripping, homie."

A few days went by, and Duke still hadn't found out who broke into his house. People were talking about it, but no one knew who did it. Biggs gave him ten birds for twenty-one grand apiece to get back on his feet. Although everyone, including Biggs, thought that he was broke, Duke was far from broke. Aunt Rose, Shawn, and La-La had money put up for him. Not to mention the money that he had stashed for hard times. Duke went on a grind, night and day for three months straight.

When he finally lay down to get a good night's rest, Duke slept for two days. As soon as he woke up, he bought two Chevy Caprices, an SS Impala, an SS Monte Carlo, a Crown Victoria, a Parrissana, a Grand Marquis, and a Suburban. He painted the Crown Victoria, one of the Caprices, and the Parriassana candy gray. With twenty-inch rims and pioneer sound system. Leaving the paint shop, Duke felt like a true baller. He drove through Parkview, eased across the speed bumps, and stepped on the gas pedal. When the mirror tinted windows slid down, tongues began to hit the pavement.

"Yea, this me."

Biggs shook his head in a displeased way as Duke drove up into the driveway.

"It look all right," he said, rubbing the paint on the hood. "Where yo Caprice at, though."

"I dropped it off when I picked this up." Biggs shook his head. "You doing too much."

Duke couldn't believe what he was hearing. Out of everyone, he just knew that Biggs would be happy for him. After taking a loss and shaking back, why wouldn't Duke be happy?

*   *   *   *

Chapter 7
From Sugar to Shit

Duke didn't have a spot in Parkview; he was still hustling out of Precious's apartment. Although she and Shamekia were best friends, Duke knew she had a strong vibe for him. Some days she would let him in and be dressed in a silk nightgown suit with nothing underneath it. He would get the urge to try Precious but quickly let it pass.

Deep down inside, Precious hated Duke because she felt that he was controlling Shamekia's life. Then again, he did something that she thought Biggs would have been done for her. Duke took Shamekia out of the projects. It was a known fact that Precious didn't like him, yet she couldn't help but admire his ways.

Duke was on his way home after dropping Shamekia off at work when he receive the call from Biggs.

"Yo."

"Where you at?"

"On my way to the crib, why? When I leave there, I'm going to Parkview."

Biggs look around at the line of cars sitting in front of Precious's building and started wishing that he had some dope.

"I'm in Parkview right now, and it is rolling off the chain."

"I'm on my way."

As Duke was making a right turn onto Lee Avenue, his car cutoff. He pulled to the side of the road and tried to restart it. It wouldn't start. He popped the hood and got out. As Duke was leaning through the window to grab his phone, a car drove up alongside him.

"Don't be bending over like that . . . I'm hot."

He spun around so fast that he hit his head on the top of the door.

"You got jokes, huh."

"Quit being so sensitive . . . I'm just playing. What's wrong with yo, heavy chevy?"

He almost asked her to take a guess. "I ran out of gas. Why, you gone let me pay you to take me to the store?"

"Don't trip, just ride with me to go pick up my girl."

"What did you say yo name was?"

"Stacy . . . an you Duke, right?"

They picked Stacy's friend Easha up off the East Side and rode through the city. Duke was really ready to get back to his car, but he went along with the flow of things. Stacy and Easha were having a good conversation in the front seat. They went from talking about cars, jewelry, clothes, and shoes to talking about whose pussy they had heard smelled bad and whose dick they knew was good.

"You two muthafuckas some freaks."

"So what, nigga, you scared of pussy. Shamekia got you wrapped right around her finger."

He looked back at Easha with a smile on his face. "We'll see."

Stacy took him to pick up his car, and they got a room at the Shoney Inn in West Monroe. Duke couldn't believe it. He had not one but two freaks in the room with him. The game was definitely starting to treat him good. He sat back on the bed smoking a blunt, watching Stacy and Easha pop triple stacks. Before long, they were tongue kissing, sucking one another's breast, and licking at each other's G-spot. Duke was loving the girl-on-girl action.

"All right, which one you want the first piece of dick," Duke asked, taking off his boxer shorts.

Stacy lay down on the bed, and Easha put her face between Stacy's legs. Duke stroked Easha from behind while she ate out

Stacy. If his phone hadn't kept ringing, they would have been in that room all night. Easha and Stacy switched positions and got the same treatment. After a quick shower, Duke hopped back in his car and took the quickest route home.

"Hello," he answered, flipping open his cell.

"The feds just hit Precious, Dubb, and U-Lay's baby momma apartment."

"What?"

The phone went dead in his ear, and he let it fall on the seat. He was a nervous wreck at the moment. The feds had just hit every spot that he would normally be at. Precious's brother drove up as Duke was pulling into his driveway.

"What the fuck going on?" he asked, getting out of the car.

He shrugged his shoulders. "I don't know."

"Well, what do you know?"

"U-Lay was gone, but they found some Pyrex jars and a scale at his baby momma crib. They ain't find shit in Dubb crib." He look down at the ground. "Precious and Biggs went to jail, though. The police supposed to been found ten rocks or some shit like that."

"All right, thank you for stopping by to let me know what's up. I'ma meet you in the hood," he told him, hopping back in the car.

Duke picked Shamekia up from work and drove straight to Parkview. He started selling dope as if nothing had happened the whole day Precious's people were bugging him to bond her out. The money that he owed Biggs wasn't being spent until Biggs told him what to do with it. Duke got word that Precious's father made her bond, so he made Biggs's bond an hour later. Once they were out, Duke laid low. He was now plotting and planning his next move because Biggs had changed on him overnight. Duke had to pay twenty-five grand for some ounces that he had already cooked up. U-Lay got busted with some dope coming back from Texas, and the first person he called was Biggs. Although, he was selling dope for Biggs, Biggs wouldn't accept his calls. U-Lay called Duke to see if he would buy his car so he could get a lawyer. Biggs didn't care about that because the money U-Lay used to go out of town belonged to him.

"U-Lay say you gone buy his car," Duke asked, taking the phone away from his ear.

"Tell that nigga I'a give him seven grand for his Lexus and another five hundred for some of his wife's pussy."

"U-Lay," he said, putting the phone to his mouth.

"Yea."

"I don't want to buy the car, but I'a loan you the money. Just send yo wife by to pick it up tomorrow."

"Don't even trip, Duke . . . I got you niggas."

"Nigga, what the—"

The phone went dead in his ear.

* * *

It was around 5:00 a.m. when Duke rolled over to look at the camera screen beside his bed. Four men were crouching down in front of the front door. He grabbed the Glock 19 and made sure one was in the head. As Duke was sliding out of bed, he saw the letters S.W.A.T. written on the back of one of the men's flak jackets. He tossed the gun behind the dresser and jumped back in the bed.

"Baby, they coming."

"Huh," Shamekia mumbled, turning over.

"They coming."

"Who coming?" she asked, sitting up.

Before he could answer her, their bedroom door was batter-rammed down. Metro Narcotic Agents came in waving assault rifles.

"Put yo hands where I can see them."

Duke raised his hands up. "I'm naked."

As soon as he reached out to be cuffed, a cuff snagged his wrist, and he was snatched out of the bed. The material things were fading, and the real picture was becoming clearer. Duke read the arrest warrant and knew U-Lay had given a statement on him. The house he had bought for him and Shamekia was being confiscated. All the cars, including the ones in the paint shop, were confiscated. Agents found seventy-five grand; two Glock 9's, and a pound of purp. Duke took the charges, and Shamekia was released. They picked her back up and kept her in jail for three days, just because they could.

The first week, Duke didn't eat or sleep. He went from having everything at his fingertips to having nothing. Everyone who had owed him money ran off when he went to jail. La-La was holding it down, but Duke was still stressing over Shamekia. Every time he called home, he heard about who was and wasn't balling; dudes who didn't have a clue about the game were the main ones with the dope now. Duke was asleep one night when someone tapped the edge of his bed. He rolled over and was surprised to see that it was Biggs. Duke hadn't seen or heard from him in over a year.

"What the fuck you in here for?"

"I got busted with sixteen birds, and these crackers finna give me football numbers. You finna go home, li'l nigga."

"Why you—"

"Just listen and shut the fuck up for a minute."

"I'ma give you my new connect down in Miami, you deserve it. Just keep it real with him, and he gonna make you rich." Biggs wrote something down on a piece of paper and gave it to Duke. "Just send me fifty grand when you get home."

Biggs left before Duke could ask any more questions.

Chapter 8
Who Gone Stop Me Now

After being on lockdown for seventeen months, Duke had a new outlook in life. So much had happened to him in the last year. People that he never thought would change switched and turned their backs on him. It was as if everyone thought that he was never coming home. Duke was in his own world until he heard the honking of a horn.

"Get out the street befo I run yo ass over," the driver of the Cadillac threatened, swerving around him.

Duke was about to curse him out, but instead he smiled and kept walking. Shawn was sitting in a plastic lawn chair when he cut across her grass. With his hands over her eyelids, Duke whispered in her ear, "You love me."

"Who the—"

"Guess," he replied, swaying from side to side.

Shawn spun around like a wild bull and knocked the chair up against the house.

"Boy, quit playing so dam much."

Duke fell over laughing. "I thought I was gone have to fight yo crazy ass."

"When you came home, jailbird?"

"'Bout twenty minutes ago."

"The man dropped your car off yesterday, and niggas been ridin' past here all day long."

Duke saw the white-on-white 745 and knew who it was for. Shawn's 470 Lexus truck was parked behind it.

"That's for me, or you been tricking off my money?" he asked, pointing at the Beemer.

"That's Conrad's, and he need to come get that hot-ass car."

Duke touched her on the stomach. "You done got fat."

"If your god brother buys you a business and gave you six figures, you can be me. What the hell is this you got on?" she asked, pulling at his shirt.

Duke looked down at the Wrangler jeans and Riddell tennis shoes. "Somebody stole my clothes and left me this."

Shawn took him into the house and up a cherrywood stairwell. Duke could tell that she had spent a nice piece of money out of his stash. Shawn stopped dead in her tracks when she saw the look on his face.

"Yep, I use some of yo money, and I don't care if you get mad. Duke, you left me with 180 grand. You know dam well I wasn't just gonna hold that shit."

Duke wasn't the least bit mad about her spending the money. While he was in jail, his commissary account was always fat, and so was everyone else's that he used to use.

Shawn opened the door to a storage room and took a step back. "Just like you left it."

He put his arm around her neck. "I don't know what I would do without you."

"Repay me by staying out of trouble for a change."

"Well, let me get fresh, then," Duke said, picking through piles of clothing still bearing price tags.

He finally settled on a blue-and-gray Prada shorts set with matching dress shoes. As Duke lay back in the shell-shaped tub, his thoughts came back to when he had to wait in line for a shower. Jail was a different world, and people who haven't been there wouldn't understand what he had gone through. Shawn was standing at the top of the stairs when he opened the bathroom door.

"I'a have to have you if you weren't my brother."

They both fell out laughing. Shawn had tears in her eyes because it had been so long since they were face-to-face. Duke didn't want her to come visit him, so she sent him pictures twice a month.

"Can I have my keys?" he asked, holding out his hand.

Shawn opened the garbage bag sitting beside the bathroom door and gave him a bulletproof vest, an MP5 with two extra clips, and a set of keys.

"The green keys for the townhouse that I bought you. I got extra keys in case you lose those."

Duke kept his hand out and didn't say a word.

"You ain't changed, but I still love you."

"I love you too, big sis."

"Uh-huh . . . here," she said, passing him the pound Ziploc bag that she had been concealing behind her back.

She gave him a kiss on the forehead, and Duke made his way out the door.

"You going chase them hoes, huh."

"Yep, hoes need love too."

He snatched the cover off the car and took a step back. A '96 SS Impala, bowling ball black, Gucci interior, and matching ragtop. The grille, trimmings, and 22-inch Asanti rims were dipped in gold. After activating the remote start, Duke got in, turned the music up sky high, and pulled out of the driveway.

*   *   *   *

Shawn was the brains behind Duke's striving force. She didn't get involved with the drug dealing, but Shawn managed his money better than any accountant ever could. Being that they grew up ruff, she learned to save, if nothing else. Therefore, when Duke put money in her hands, she would wash it clean—not once but twice! When he went away, Shawn was more hurt than anyone, because Duke took care of the family. Nothing was too big or small for him. So in return, she made sure that he received money orders, pictures, magazines, books, and letters twice a month. Some people said she did too much for him, but Shawn felt that it wasn't enough. She clicked the troff, and heard Duke coming down her street. Shawn knew it was him because he was playing the same song before he left.

"Nigga, turn that shit down . . . we ain't in the hood," she said, meeting him at the garage door.

"My bad, Ms. Too Good for the Hood, everybody ain't able." He passed her a piece of paper. "I need you to send Biggs fifty grand and use the rest to buy everything on that list. Here, take this back," he said, passing her the Ziploc bag.

"I'm finna start charging you for everything you put in my name."

"Call me," he responded, backing out of her driveway.

Shawn was too happy to see Duke, but she was scared of what he was up to.

*　　*　　*　　*

"Hello?"

He could hear a lot of noise in the background. "Can I speak to La-La?"

"Hold on . . . La-La, telephone," the woman called out and set the phone down.

"Hello, who is this?"

"You sound kinda busy, do you want me to call you back?"

"Don't start cursing me out, boy. You already havn't call or wrote me in over a month."

Duke got out of the car and walked over to the front door. "Come outside."

"If I didn't know better—"

La-La swung the door open, and her heart started racing. She fell into his open arms, planting kisses all over his face. "Quit playing with me," she said, bear-hugging him.

"You ready to go?"

La-La looked back over his shoulder and saw the Impala sitting in the middle of the street with its blinkers on.

"We having a baby shower for my sister right now."

He pulled back from her embrace. "Call me when you ready, then."

"Why you leaving?" She wrapped both arms back around his waist. "Come inside for a few minutes."

"I just came home, baby girl. You know like I know I'm about to put my foot on these niggas."

"Well, you wanna go get your money. I got it put up at my grandma crib."

"Finish enjoying yourself and call me tonight."

La-La touched the front of his shorts. "Don't go give my dick away because I'ma be the first to get that." She looked in his eyes. "You know I know you . . . now give me a kiss."

*   *   *   *

Turning into Parkview Apartments, the SS Impala came to a slow crawl, Yokohoma tires coming to a stop at the guard shack. The guard peeped into the car, leaning in the driver's side window.

"Who you going to see?"

"My girl."

"Like I know—"

"Shamekia."

The guard pondered the name for a moment. "Oh, you mean the dark-skin cutie, short hair, got a li'l tattoo on her back, live in 109."

"Dam, you watching my girl like that."

"I thought she was Li'l Daddy's girl."

"Oh yea."

The guard agreed by nodding his head and walking back to the shack. Duke turned the music back up and watched the hatred jump out of the haters as he drove past. Kids were running back and forth with no shoes and shirts on. It was definitely summertime. Duke had to swerve from left to right, avoiding piles of trash and broken bottles.

"The hood ain't changed," he said, crossing the speed bumps.

Shamekia was the first person that Duke saw when he drove up to Building 18. She was leaning against an S-Type Jaguar tongue kissing some young-looking dude. He backed the car in beside them and took out his cell phone.

"Hello," a familiar voice answered.

"Where ya, girl?"

"Who is this?"

"Duke."

"Hold on . . . Shamekia, girl I know you hear me. Telephone, it's Duke."

Shamekia stood on the sidewalk, watching the Jag pull off. "You said that was Duke."

"Nah . . . ya daddy, hoe."

She ran into the house to grab the phone. "What?"

"What's up?"

"I'm sitting in front the building with Precious."

Duke lit a blunt and took a long drag. "You must of thought I wasn't never coming home."

"Shid, you ain't told me otherwise."

"Well, I heard that you and li'l daddy fucking, tell me otherwise."

He knew she would lie—it's human nature. Especially when someone feels you are only assuming or going off he or she say.

"Baby, don't start with me today. You already know you my one and only."

Duke opened the car door to get out. "You must think I'm dumb or some shit."

"I ain't gotta lie to you, Duke. You acting like you my daddy or something, better yet—"

He dropped the phone on the seat and closed the door.

"Hello, hello . . . I know this nigga ain't hung up on me, Precious. Duke done lost his dam mind."

Shamekia was so mad that she didn't see the look on Precious's face.

"Questioning me like he my daddy or some shit. They should give his ass fifty years."

Duke turned to face her with a smile on his face. "Nigga told me that you was a trifling hoe, but I didn't believe him. You stole twenty grand from me when I went to jail and look at you, you ain't shit."

Shamekia was shook, shocked, and froze with a puzzled look on her face. She couldn't believe he was sitting in the chair in front of her. Shamekia's words fell out of her mouth.

"I ain't . . . I know—"

"Save that shit for one of them lame-ass niggas because it ain't gone work on me. The twenty Gs you stole was worth the look on yo face."

Duke grabbed the phone off the seat and hopped in the car. "Hello?"

"We waiting on you at Mom's crib. Where you at?"

He saw La-La's number light up on the display screen.

"We gone holla tomorrow." He hung up on Conrad to click over to the other line. "You ready?"

"Should I be?"

Duke sped out of Parkview and headed for the highway. "You better be."

*   *   *   *

After picking up La-La from her sister's house, Duke stopped by Super Walmart. As they were walking through the entrance doors, La-La was almost run over by a group of men.

"Say, playboy"—Duke pulled La-La to the side—"you and the Three Stooges need to watch where the fuck you going."

Everyone watching thought that a fight was about to break out, but one of the men extended his hand.

"Dam, Duke, that's you."

"Baby, go inside and wait for me over by the Frozen section." He turned back to the three gentlemen standing in front of him. "If it ain't Mann . . . where yo books at, schoolboy."

"I see you still got jokes, huh. Yo whole click roll for me. Ask yo li'l brother how I get down, he'ca tell you."

Duke thought about walking back out to the car to get his pistol. Then again, he could just slap the taste out of Mann's mouth. Instead of doing the obvious, Duke made himself smile.

"I'ma see you around, hustla," he responded before walking off.

Steam was blowing out of Duke's ears as he drove home. Duke just couldn't understand it. Before he went to jail, Mann was a high school nerd. Out of all the people in Monroe, Mann had to choose Conrad and Diron to work for him. La-La was wondering what they were doing on the north side, until Duke drove up to a newly built townhouse. The garage rose up, and he drove in, shutting it as soon as the car was in park. He popped the trunk and got out of the car. La-La knew something was wrong because he hadn't said a word since they left Walmart.

"Hey"—she tapped Duke on the shoulder—"I'ma give you a dollar for each one of your thoughts."

"I'm just thinking about life."

She could tell that there was more to it than he was letting on, but she didn't want to spoil the moment.

"You know I love you regardless, huh."

He bit La-La on the back of her neck. "Go shower . . . I'ma roll up the weed and fix something to eat."

La-La pushed the door open and stood in the doorway. Duke was surprised to see that the house had been furnished. Everything was still covered in plastic, including the plush white carpet. She kicked the sandals off her feet before stepping into the house.

"You sho you just came home." She looked back at Duke. "I'm saying, somebody besides me must really love you."

"My godsister did this shit . . . Aunt Roz them love to spend my money."

Duke went into the kitchen, and La-La began snatching the plastic off the furniture. While he busied himself cooking, La-La took a shower. She came out of the bedroom a while later with five rolled-up blunts and their drinks. The first glass classy drink had Duke pissy drunk.

"I think I'ma have to finish the cooking. You cook like you gone burn the food, and I'm hungry as hell," La-La told him, falling over laughing.

T-bone steaks, Jiffy Cornbread, mac and cheese, and rice and gravy. He wanted to have sex, but his mind was on money.

"Baby, I'm horny," La-La replied, as if reading his mind.

He patted his lap. "I am too, but come here."

She sat on his lap and laid her head on his shoulder.

"What I'ma do with you?"

"You better be with me until I get old," she stated, raising her head to look in his face.

"You remember what we talked about in my letters?"

"What, about the dope? I told you that my friend Tina can help too."

"That's cool, but right now, you are all I need."

"When we leaving, then."

He slid his hand under the silk nightgown and felt that she wasn't wearing any panties.

"Let me show you how much I miss and love you first. Then we can talk about whatever you want."

*   *   *   *

Conrad, Hotboy, Will, and Shagg were standing in the alleyway behind Mann's house. They'd been planning on robbing him for over a year, and today all the pieces had fallen into place. Now that Duke was home, his services were no longer needed.

"Look, we gone kick the door in and tie everybody up. We get the money and be gone in fifteen minutes max."

"You sho this gone work?" Will asked for insurance.

"Have I ever failed you?"

Conrad peeped through a side window and saw moment in the kitchen "look."

"I see four," Hotboy replied, throwing up four fingers.

"They got money and dope on the table," Shagg said, peering over Hotboy's shoulder.

"Shush . . . you gone let them know that we out here."

Will shook his head, watching the blue GS Lexus back into the driveway.

"I thought you said that Regina would be gone," he said, looking at Hotboy.

"Fuck her, we too far gone to just turn back."

Regina popped the trunk and got out of the car. She reached down in the trunk and felt something pressing against her lower back.

"Shh . . . shh . . . shh . . . scream and you dead."

"Her go my—"

"Bitch, shut up!" Conrad demanded through clenched teeth. "Open the front door for me."

The old wooden porch squeaked as if at the point of giving in, with the weight of all five people on it at one time.

"Somebody on yo porch."

"Put that shit away while I go see who it is."

Mann reached out to unlock the deadbolt and heard keys being stuck in the lock.

"Hey ba—"

Hotboy hit him in the face with the butt of the AR-15, and Conrad pushed Regina to the floor.

"If you move, I'ma kill you first."

One of the men stuck his hand under the table, and three muted shots rang out. He fell over facefirst on the table, dead as a doorknob.

"Who next?" Conrad asked, looking around.

"You think you gone rob me and not wear mask. You niggas dead."

"Clear the table off," Hotboy commanded, taking charge. "I'm only asking once . . . Where is it?"

"I just reused." He hunched his shoulders. "That's it, nigga."

As if on cue, Conrad shot Mann in the head twice and six times in the chest. Regina jumped up screaming and ran for the door. Hotboy grabbed her around the neck and choke-slammed her.

"Bitch . . . where the money at, befo I choke the life out yo nasty ass."

"In back," she coughed, gasping for air.

Conrad shot the other two men as Hotboy took Regina to the back of the house. He followed her to the laundry room and saw her easing over by the back door.

"Try me."

Regina realized that she was in a no-win situation, and the tears began to flow.

"I'm the one who told you that the connect would be here today, why you wanna hurt me, Hotboy?"

"All right, where the money at?"

"It's over there."

"Just get it for me, and I'ma let you go."

Conrad, Shagg, and Will walked up just as Regina opened the dryer, revealing a built-in safe. She twisted the dial from right to left and swung the metal door open.

"I op—"

Hotboy put two bullets in the back of Regina's head as she was about to stand up. Her lifeless body slumped over, leaning up against the washing machine.

"You got blood all over the money," Conrad scream, looking in the safe.

"Fuck it, get it and let's go."

*   *   *

Duke rolled over to grab the blunt out of the ashtray and saw La-La standing in the doorway watching him.

"You finally decided to wake up, huh. I fix your favorite, so get out that bed." She gave him a piece of breakfast pork chop. "They have something on the news about a multiple homicide early this morning. It should be about to come back on."

He took a quick shower and joined La-La at the bar in the kitchen, just as the twelve o'clock news was coming on.

"Four males and a female were found brutally murdered inside of a Southside home after daybreak this morning. No names are available, and no arrests have been made at this point in time. There is not much to go on, but there are signs of a drug deal gone bad."

He clicked the TV off and couldn't believe what he had just seen. This really made him know that life was too short; you could be here today and gone tomorrow.

"You remember dude who almost ran you over in Walmart last night?"

"Yea, why?"

"That was his house that them people got murdered at."

La-La was looking as if she didn't catch on, and Duke didn't feel like explaining. He ate the rest of the breakfast, rolled a few more blunts, and got dressed to leave.

Chapter 9
Getting Plugged

The call was made to the connect that Biggs had given him, and Duke was given instruction to fly down to Miami, Florida. He picked La-La up from her grandmother's house, put his car in Shawn's garage, and had her drop them off at the airport. Flying wasn't one of his strong points, but he had to make an exception for this. The money belt strapped to his waist gave him all the inspiration he needed. Two hours after taking flight, the plane came to a screeching halt at a hangar in Miami, Florida, at Miami International Airport. "Tourist" was written all over their face as they made their way through the airport.

"I'm here," he said, pressing the button on his Nextel phone.

"Someone should be waiting on you by the curb," the voice told him.

Duke was beginning to think that he was being set up. The feeling in his stomach was getting worse by the minute. A black Benz drove up to the curb, and the driver got out.

"Duke."

"Yea," he replied with a skeptical look on his face.

"Get in, we need to get going."

The driver took the interstate and got off on the first exit. He drove down a side street, made two left turns, and a right turn, before getting back on the interstate. La-La put her hand over his and gave a firm squeeze. Duke knew what she was thinking because the same thing had come across his mind. At the moment, though, money was the only thing on his mind. Life had dealt him many ups and downs, good and bad times; yet for some strange reasons, he felt that these things were about to change. The car came to a stop in front of a massive structure. Duke and La-La were led to an elevator in the corner of the twelve-car garage. Duke had a million things on his mind when the elevator door came open. A neatly dressed man and two gorrilla-looking men were waiting.

"The lovely lady downstairs," he told the driver. "Duke, step off the elevator and put your hands on the wall."

Duke was searched and relieved of the money belt around his waist. He thought about protesting, but this didn't seem like the best time to argue. The two men took him to a room where he was to be left and locked inside. After a few minutes, he heard someone twisting the doorknob. Duke stood to his feet.

"No one's going to hurt you . . . have a seat. Believe me, you're in good hands."

"This a nice crib," he said, trying to make small talk.

He studied Duke's facial expression for a moment before pulling out a cigar from the breast pocket of his suit.

"Have one," he said, extending one in Duke's direction.

He reached out to grab the cigar and was surprised when the man didn't give it to him.

"I'm going to give you one try, and if you fuck me, I'm going to kill you." He leaned his head to the side, looking at Duke from that angle. "The money inside that belt is enough for fifteen kilos . . . so good to you."

Duke did a quick calculation and saw that he was paying ten thousand a kilo.

"If you don't mind my asking, how am I supposed to get my dope back to Monroe?"

"If you are willing to pay for it, anything is possible."

"I understand that, but—"

"All of my product is 100 percent, OK. You can make three, maybe four, kilos off of one. I advise you to have Shawn buy you a house by the beach because this is your first and last time coming here. Have a nice flight."

Duke didn't know what to say. He was wondering how this man knew about Shawn.

"What am I supposed to call you?"

He lit both of their cigars. "Dre."

*   *   *

Duke was sweating bullets as he made his way down the exit ramp; him being nervous wasn't the half of it for him. La-La, on the other hand, seemed to be made for this type of work. They made it outside and had a cab take them to Shawn's house, where La-La got out. Duke sat back in the cab staring at the ceiling on the way to his townhouse. He knew that if he made it home, it was on like never before; but if he got caught, he'd get a hell of a lot of time. Shawn saw La-La backing the Impala out of the garage and knew Duke was up to no good. She stood in the doorway watching the Impala until its taillights were out of sight. La-La stopped by the 2- hour head shop to pick up the supplies that Duke would need and bought a Vision ware set from Walmart.

Duke began cutting the dope around three in the morning. La-La sat at the table breaking the powder down. Most people used baby sugar, but Duke didn't want the dope to taste so sweet. His substitute was Inositol sold in powder form at GNC stores. He also had La-La pick up some Mannitol; blending Inositol with lidocaine covers up the sweetness in the Inositol and replaces the numbing effect lost from cutting the dope. La-La mixed the dope and cut in a punch bowl to fluff it up. He still had to show her how to separate the loose powder and shake from the solid pieces. For every twenty grams of coke, he added twenty grams of cut. The hardest part of the cutting process is to recompress the dope. Duke would have never gotten the job done if it hadn't been for the small boxlike object that La-La got from the head shop. She sprayed Acetone on the dope to moisten it like he taught her, and Duke use the boxlike object to compress the dope into a rectangular block. He then used Ziploc bags, Saran wrap, and duct tape to package the dope for distribution.

It was after ten in the morning when they finally finished the cutting process. La-La fell asleep on the counter in the kitchen, and he had to carry her to bed.

Duke was wrapping up the last kilo when his cell phone started vibrating.

"Yea."

"Duke, you back husting?"

He ripped the tape with his teeth. "No."

"Quit lying all the dam time, boy. I know you too dam well to believe that you're investing six figures and ain't got shit to fall back on."

"What more do you want me to say?"

Aunt Roz shook the phone because she couldn't believe what she was hearing. After promising her that he was finished with the dope while on lockdown, Duke couldn't quit. Although he didn't admit it, she knew he was back to hustling.

"Well, if you know what's good for you, you'll be over here by twelve o'clock. And don't make me come over to your house."

"OK, OK . . . bye."

Duke was dog tired after cutting and packaging dope for almost eight hours straight. He really didn't have the energy to make it to Aunt Roz's house, but Duke couldn't say no. There was no way in the world he would let her come over to his house and see it the way that it was at that very moment. He put Pine-Sol and bleach on everything in the kitchen. Once everything was spotless, he took the time to fix La-La breakfast.

"Get up, sleepyhead," he said, clicking the room light on.

La-La rolled over and pulled the covers over her head. "No . . . baby, I'm tired."

"I'm about to go," he told her, setting the tray on the nightstand.

"Unt-uh, get in this bed and get some sleep."

Duke sat down on the bed beside her and rubbed his hand up and down the curves of her body.

"I need you to stay here and tape the bricks up two at a time while I go see what the hell Aunt Roz wants."

"Bye," she said and pulled the cover back over her head.

Duke took a shower, got dressed as quick as possible, and was out the door before La-La could protest. He made a stop at the first dumpster he saw to get rid of the garbage bags in his trunk.

Chapter 10
Setting Examples

The house was completely dark when Duke pushed the door open. No cars were in the driveway, and no one was out front in the yard. He hit a table and flipped the light on.

"Surprise!"

He swung the MP5 from behind his back and burst out laughing. Aunt Roz didn't find any humor in a gun being pointed at her.

"We can't surprise his crazy ass no mo . . . he be done killed us. Go put that dam gun in yo car."

Now he knew why there weren't any cars in the driveway; they were packed on the backside of the house. It made him feel good to see Aunt Roz living in a thousand-dollar house. It let him know that he was on his business. Duke was staring off in the sky and didn't see Conrad, Hotboy, and Will creep up, with buckets of water. By the time he turned back around, it was too late.

"You muthafuckas losing yo minds . . . this Gucci," he told them, dodging the water.

"Here, take this as a token of appreciation."

Everyone passed him a thick white envelope and gave Duke a hug. The thought of where it came from never did cross his mind; he had plans for this money.

"Where the work at, Conrad. Mann gave y'all some bricks befo he got killed."

Conrad looked at Hotboy. "It's gone . . . why, you must got something."

"Yea, I got, like, thirty birds or some shit."

"How much you want for all thirty?" Diron ask, walking up with a tray of classy drinks.

"Fifteen grand a piece."

"What?" Conrad grabbed one from Diron. "You must got a fire-ass connect giving you work for cheap."

"I just want everybody to get money, li'l bro."

"We going half on all that, then. Don't sell nobody else no dope, and we gone buy everything you got."

Duke wanted to tell his god-brothers to slow down, but it was too late. How could he tell them not to hustle and he was headfirst back in the streets.

"Call me tonight, and I'ma tell you where to meet me at, Conrad. Hotboy, take a ride with me."

*   *   *

Raindrops were beating down on top of the car as the Impala skated through Plantation Apartments.

"You remind me so much of myself, and I love that about you, but I'ma get right to the point. Everything about to change, and I need to know if you're ready."

Duke took a long drag on the blunt before passing it to Hotboy. "You about to see mo money in the next six months, then you done ever seen in yo whole life. You gone be my right hand—"

"What about yo god-brothers?"

"Just listen . . . I'm calling the shots around here. Everybody gone get money, but I want you to get money with me. You was the only nigga to pick up a pen and write me while I was on lockdown. In the next thirty days, we gone take over Monroe. Then we gone take the south."

Hotboy didn't know what Duke was planning to do next, but he knew it was something big.

"What if niggas don't respect the come up?"

Duke saw Snooppy peeping out the window, and he got out of the car, Hotboy did the same.

"I'm willing to die for what I want. I can only hope that everyone else feels the same as me."

Snooppy opened the door, looking as sexy as he could remember. Standing five feet seven, with long hair, light-brown eyes, and high cheekbones. Milk-chocolate skin complexion with bow legs, you had to look twice when she walk past you. The first time Duke saw her, he had to have her. She played hard to get, but he eventually won her over.

"Yo food in the oven, and if yo boy want some, he can fix it himself."

Before Duke could put her in her place, Snooppy walked off. This was one of the reasons why she would never be number one in his life. Snooppy was too sexy for her own good.

"Brang yo nappy-headed ass back here," he screamed down the hallway.

He took a moment before realizing she wasn't coming back. Duke knew what had to be done. It was no secret that he went hard on all of his women. The fact that they were all dimes didn't matter.

"I'a be right back," he told Hotboy.

Hotboy started laughing because he knew what was about to happen. He walked through the bedroom door, and Snooppy was sitting on the edge of the bed polishing her toenails. Duke closed the door and slapped the nail polish out of her hand.

"Bitch, who you think you is?"

"Why you tripping . . . OK, what I'm supposed to been did now?"

He slapped Snooppy so hard that she flew halfway across the room.

"When I call you, I don't give a fuck why or what you doing, you better come see what I want."

She wrapped both arms around his leg. "I'm sorry, baby . . . I messed up. I'm just mad that you didn't come straight home to me."

He wanted to feel sympathy for her, but his heart wouldn't allow it.

"When you stop loving the way I drive my ship." He lifted her head back to look in Snooppy's eyes. "You gone have to use yo own life raft to move around."

"But, baby—"

"Take your clothes off and lay on yo stomach, because I don't wanna see yo face right now."

Snoopy did as she was told, and Duke treated her like a two-dollar whore, applying pressure to her lower back and grabbing a handful of her hair. Duke pushed as deep as he could inside of her while stroking her hard and long. He used his free hand to slap her on her ass cheeks. Snooppy thought he was finished when Duke began to slow his pace, but he caught his breath and sped right back up. He felt her body shaking beneath him and rolled over, knowing she had been satisfied.

"Now go in the bathroom and clean yo self up with yo fine ass, then I want you to take yo ass back in the kitchen and fix Hotboy a plate of food."

She put a hand on her wide hip. "Why he—"

"Go do what the fuck I told yo hardheaded ass, dam."

"OK, I'm sorry."

She gave him a peck on the cheek and went in the bathroom. Duke lay back on the bed pondering his next move. It was time to make a big move if he was planning on taking over. The sound of his phone ringing broke Duke's concentration.

"Yo."

"I pick those things up . . . you ready?"

"Round everybody up and meet me at the club."

"One."

Duke took a shower and made a few more calls, before joining Snooppy and Hotboy in the living room. His food was on the table, and Hotboy was almost finished with his plate when he finally did walk in the living room.

"Snooppy," he called out, taking a seat on the couch.

"Huh."

"What we supposed to drink, Ms. Smart Mouth?"

Snooppy came running down the hallway like a track star. She went in the kitchen and came out with two glasses of ice-cold Kool-Aid. Hotboy took a glass out of her hand, and she plopped down on the couch beside Duke.

"You bet not been done spit in this?" he said, looking in the glass.

Hotboy spat the Kool-Aid he was about to swallow back in the glass.

"Boy, you know dam well I wouldn't spit in yo glass. Now gimme some," she said, taking the spoon out of his hand.

"That's why you getting so dam fat as it is . . . you too dam greedy."

"It's after six, homie," Hotboy told him, looking down at the Cartier watch on his wrist.

Snooppy grabbed Duke by the arm as he stood up to leave. "You coming home tonight?"

"Don't question me . . . question the kids at your job when you go to work in the morning," he replied, snatching his arm out of her grasp.

*   *   *

AP sat at the bar downing shots of Patron waiting for 10:00 p.m., and it was only 7:00 p.m. He had plenty of time to play around. One of the strippers came out on the stage wearing a black fishnet. AP was about to get a lap dance from her when someone knocked at the side door.

"Hold up, baby girl," he said, slapping the naked woman on her backside. "Who is it?"

"The HNIC."

AP didn't hear the response, but he still pushed the door open. He tried not to show it, but fear was dancing in his eyes. AP was old in the age department, but he was still considered a pretty boy. With gray eyes, curly hair, and a caramel complexion, he was your heartbreaking pretty boy. Duke was far from ugly, but he couldn't stand pretty niggas.

"I'm surprised to see you over this way, Duke," he said, reaching out to shake hands.

Duke shook AP's hands with his left hand and pulled out a gun with his right hand.

"Let's go in the back, or these hoes gone lose all respect for you as a man."

He saw the cold steel being pointed at him and led the way to his office without further conversation. Duke couldn't believe his luck: AP's partners in crime were conducting business over a game of pool. Everyone in the room froze except Duke when the sound of machine guns being cocked sounded off.

"As of today, you old muthafuckas have made your last dime. I'm taking over from here on out."

Leroy jumped up from his chair. "This how we eat . . . You can't—"

"Sit the fuck down before I forget you and my daddy was brothers." He took a seat on the edge of the desk. "Let me get this straight and correct me if I'm wrong. AP fronting the

Berg Jones Lane Boys, Elmore flooding South First to South Twenty-Fourth and you running everything from Wilson to Mississippi Street." Duke grabbed one of the pool sticks and broke it in half. "Y'all control the whole fucking south side. But as of today—you young punks ain't about to come up in my place of business and take nothing. If you wasn't my own flesh and blood, you would already be dead."

With the speed of light, he hit Leroy in the temple with the gun. "Hold him down," he told Hotboy, and Will grabbed the broken pool stick. "I want you to tell yo partners I said don't fuck with me."

Blood squirted everywhere and on everyone when he stabbed Leroy in the eye with the pool stick. He squealed like a pig when Duke twisted the stick in his eye socket.

"You want some?" he asked, pointing the bloody stick at Elmore and AP.

"No," they replied in unison.

Hotboy slammed Leroy on the floor, and Duke put his foot on Leroy's neck. "Now, I'ma spare you yo life because we got the same bloodline," Duke told him with a smile.

*   *   *   *

Shawn bought Duke a house and a condo in Miami. He made so much money in the first three months after the takeover that he quit counting it. Dre was trying to get him to take some keys on cosignment, but he politely refuse to take them. Although, he knew the royal treatment would cost him before long, three times out of a month Duke was on a plane to Miami. When he returned home, the dope was cut, recompressed, and sold without a problem. Everyone he dealt with was treated fairly, family or not. But sometimes treating someone fairly gives them the sense of wanting to get over. Bo was a prime example of how family will try to get over on you. Even though Bo had stolen from him once before, Duke still refused to completely turn his back on him. The last straw came when he broke into one of Duke's stash houses and stole sixty grand. Duke wasn't mad about the money; he was mad when he found out who had stolen the money. This made him realize that he had to set an example for all future references. Conrad and Hotboy picked Bo up off the streets and continued to feed him dope like Duke had told them to do.

Everyone was sitting at the picnic tables when Duke pulled up to the hideaway. The hideaway was really a couple of barns and a huge wooden house sitting on thirty acres of land. No one knew why Duke wanted to meet, but they knew it was an emergency, because he woke every one up at one in the morning.

Diron was the first to speak up. "I know dam well you ain't wake me up to kill no crackhead. That nigga ain't—"

"I love you to death . . .will kill and die for you, but I'a kill you too if you steal from me." Duke slammed his fist down on the table. "That goes for everybody, and I mean this from the heart. Now let's go talk to Bo."

They searched the barn and found Bo in one of the back stalls smoking his life away. When the stall door flew open, he dropped the glass dick on the floor.

"Oop," he said, looking at the shattered glass.

"Get up."

He stood up and fell again. "Cuzz, what's going on?"

"Give me my dope back that you done smoke for the last two weeks."

He saw the pistol in Duke's hand and realize that this could be the end.

"Please . . . please, I'm sick, cuzz." He crawled over to Duke and wrapped his arms around one of Duke's legs. "I can work it off, li'l cuzz. Conrad, tell him I can work it off."

Duke knew killing Bo wasn't right, but nothing in life was right. In life you have to make harsh decisions, and sometimes the right decision isn't made. Bo's head jerked back when the gun went off. Duke saw the hurt in Diron's eyes, but his heart told him that he made the right choice.

"Clean this shit up and dump the body in the swamps."

Chapter 11
Neva Eva Change

Hustling is hustling. Duke didn't have to sell a crumb, and the money was still pouring in. All he had to do was buy the dope, get it back to Monroe, and ship it out. Upstate hustlers were paying thirty grand a key without a complaint. In one year, Duke made so much money that Shawn had him open up numerous safe deposit boxes. That wasn't counting the money she already had put up for him, the money La-La had stashed at her grandmother's house or the money he put up for himself. Duke knew that he could die or go to jail any day, but he was prepared. His kids or his kids' kids would never work a day in their lives. Not many people could actually say that they had made a million dollars from hustling. Duke took the hand he was dealt and feneesed a win out of it.

La-La was waiting at the townhouse with the dope when he made it back to Monroe. She jumped into his arms and wrapped her legs around his waist as soon as he walked through the front door.

"How was your trip?" she asked, planting kisses all over his face.

"Tiring . . . been smoking, drinking, and partying all weekend. But other than that, I'm cool. Why, how you been?"

"I was worried when you didn't call me over the weekend. Oh yea, Aunt Roz been calling her every five minutes looking for you. I don't know what the heck is going on."

"Here," he said, passing her his cell phones.

Duke clicked the big-screen TV on and grabbed the house phone.

"Hello."

"Hey, you called me."

"What the hell is wrong with you?"

He clicked the TV off. "What now?"

"I know like hell you don't think that I'm crazy. My son is ridin' around in a brand-new 600 Benz, Duke. You got them out there selling yo shit and yo—"

"They was in the game when I came home. Don't call me blaming me because you wasn't on yo Ps and Qs."

"If something happen to them, I promise—"

"I gotta go," he said, cutting her off.

He hung up the phone and lay back on the couch. If it wasn't one thing, it was another. La-La came out of the kitchen with a plate of food and a glass of orange juice.

"Baby, what's wrong?" she asked, seeing the look on his face.

"Just thinking about the shit I need to do."

"You know we supposed to meet with the realtor today and go see that house. You also told me to remind you to open those laundry mats and stores."

Duke realized that La-La knew a lot of his business as he sat back listening to her. She saw him cut dope and count money. Before he let her leave him, Duke would kill La-La. When he came home, Duke made her quit her job. He didn't like the idea of making her depend on him, but it guaranteed him control over her life. La-La knew about his other women, but she paid it no mind. Maybe because he came home to her every night, except the nights he wasn't in town.

*   *   *

Shagg was smoking his morning blunt, sitting outside his house, when Duke came flying down the street in his Impala. He pulled into the driveway and hopped out, looking like a true-blue millionaire.

"You the hardest nigga I know to catch up with. I been trying to catch up with you all weekend."

"Let me hit that," he said, taking a seat next to Shagg. "I been on my biz, cousin."

Shagg waved to La-La out in the car. "You got the wifey ridin' with you this morning, huh. Must be nice."

"Is that me?" Duke asked, looking at the duffel bag sitting beside Shagg's chair.

"Yea, you got that for me."

"Come by the house in about an hour and pick that up."

"I'm on my way."

Duke tossed the duffel bag in the backseat before sliding in behind the wheel. He drove to his storage house to switch cars before heading over to Shawn's house. La-La helped count and package the money from Shagg, Conrad, Diron, Will, and Hotboy. Duke hid the money inside the secret compartments built in the Suburban and put in a call to Miami.

"Car Town . . . how may I help you?"

"Yes, I purchased a Chevy Suburban from you a few weeks back, and I'm having problems with the motor."

"Hold one moment, please."

She put Duke on hold to consult with her boss.

"Mr. Drego."

"Yes, Maliah," he answered, looking up from his desk.

"I have a gentleman on line 1, says he bought a Suburban from us a few weeks back. He's having problems with the motor."

Dre smiled. "Tell him to fax over his information, and we'll send a carrier to pick it up."

* * *

"La-La, hurry up," he hollered up the steps.

"I'm coming, baby . . . I'm sure."

"Pain is love."

She grabbed the purse off the bedroom door. "Well, if that's the case, punish me."

"You got that, but right now, I need you to hurry up. I told you I got somebody to see."

"I'm ready."

Duke looked back and saw LaLa coming down the steps and did a double take. She was wearing a Gucci catsuit, matching three-inch pumps, sunglasses, a scarf around her neck, and a book bag–sized purse draped over her shoulder. She didn't look nothing like the wild young girl he had met four years ago; this was a grown woman standing before him. La-La put her arms around his neck, and Duke cupped her ass cheeks, lifting her off her feet.

"You know I love it when you do that . . . I'm already getting moist."

"Nope, we finna go."

"Please, just five minutes."

Duke shook his head no. "What did I say?"

"OK . . . we gotta pick up Tina first."

"She can't ride in my truck, unt-uh. You can go pick her up and meet me at the mall."

"Can I drive the Impala, then?"

"Go head, but don't scratch up my paint," he told her, walking out the door.

*   *   *

Snooppy was just stepping out of the shower when he walked through the front door. Before the door was shut, she was all over him. *Dam, this hoe fine,* he thought to himself while looking at her wet naked body. As he was about to get in the bed, his phone rang. Snooppy tried to stop him, but he answered it anyway.

"Yo," he answered, slapping Snooppy's hand.

"Baby, where you parked at?"

"I'm gonna run a li'l late . . . but twenty minutes."

"Call me when you get here, then," she said, riding around the mall parking lot.

"OK."

Duke quit fighting Snooppy once he hung the phone up. She took him in her mouth and gave him deep throat like it had been legalized. Using pure head game, she put her hands on his kneecaps and went to work. The licking, slurping, and sucking had Duke digging his toes in the carpet. Snooppy felt him throbbing inside her warm mouth and took it out, rubbing him against her face. Duke sat up to see why she stopped, and they made intense eye contact. She gave him a sly grin before putting it back in her mouth. Duke took a quick shower and was out the door.

Following behind them, La-La met him at the mall entrance, and he watched the women shop. It didn't make sense to him why she searched through every store for a bargain, and La-La had enough money to buy whatever she wanted. After going in and out of almost every store in the mall, Duke was ready to leave. As they were walking out of the food court, he tapped La-La on the shoulder.

"What, you ready?" she asked, turning around.

Her eyes caught sight of the red velvet box in his hand, and La-La didn't know what to do. She almost fainted, seeing the size of the pink diamond. Her mouth wouldn't stay closed long enough to utter a word, but Tina was always more than willing to speak for her.

"Now I see why the hoe don't do shit but stay at home. You done spoil my girl."

"I don't spoil her . . . she just get what she want and need," he said, mugging Tina. "Baby I'm finna go, because I got some shit to do."

"You coming home at a decent time."

Duke knew she was asking him that to confirm it in front of Tina.

"What I told you about that. Monkeys put on a show to impress the people watching, and you don't look like no monkey."

La-La let her head drop, and Duke put his finger under her chin to lift it back up.

"Give me a kiss and don't forget to pick my clothes up from the cleaners."

A green 850 BMW pulled alongside Duke as he was getting in his truck. He paid it no mind at first but she just kept staring. Duke stopped what he was doing and went over to the car.

"Do you like what you see?" he asked, tapping on the window.

"It all depends."

He looked down and saw a three-ring wedding band on her finger.

"Where yo husband at while you sitting here flirting with me?"

"He's somewhere being him, why?"

"Because you being you, huh."

"I think you might need this one day," she said, handing him a card.

Duke flipped the card over. "Is it business or pleasure I'ma need you for?"

"I wrote my private number on the back . . . call me when you get a chance."

Duke got in his truck and let the window down. "I might just do that, Mrs. Washington."

*　　*　　*

The 28-inch rims were spinning nonstop when the Jolley Rancher–green EXT drove up. The Lamborghini doors rose up, and Duke hopped out fresh to death. The world was his, and no one could tell him differently. All heads turned when Duke walked through the doors of Bayshun Hair and Nail Salon.

"Sis-in-law," he said, hugging Shelby's neck. "Hotboy and Boo made it yet?"

"Yea, they back there in the office."

Duke scanned the faces in attendance to pick out a victim. "Who is that?" he asked, whispering in Shelby's ear.

"You gone quit pussy hunting in my shop, boy. Where in that house whore of yours at?"

"She should be pulling up at any moment, why, you gone tell one me?"

"Go in the back before I curse you out and hurt your li'l feelings today."

"I hear ya . . . Make me send Hotboy up here."

Duke bumped the chair of a light-skinned female on his way to the Coke machine. She waited to see if he was going to apologize, but Duke kept walking to the back of the shop.

"Excuse you," she said, rolling her eyes.

"Nah, excuse you," he responded with a smile.

"Hey, Duke," a voice said from behind him.

He looked back and was face-to-face with Snooppy.

"What's up?"

"Can I get a hug or something?"

Duke looked back at the light-skinned female and laughed. "Don't make me clown in public."

"You know she with me, huh," Snooppy told Duke, looking over his shoulder.

"Well, let's go talk to her, then."

Duke took a seat next to the light-skinned female. "Snooppy said you like it from the back."

"I don't know who you think you talking to, but you got the wrong one."

Snooppy was about to speak, but the look Duke gave her made Snooppy change her mind.

"What's yo name, Ms. Attitude?"

"Dee, why?"

"I'ma show you why . . . Shelby."

"What, Duke?"

"Ms. Dee over here say she paying for everybody's hair-do."

"I don't know about these other hoes, but you can't buy me with your li'l games and shit," she said, leaning over, whispering in his ear.

"Oh, yeah, seen shit yet. Snooppy gone take you to pick up some Vickies, and I'ma see you tonight." He gave Snooppy a kiss on the cheek before whispering in her ear. "Fix your face and do what you good at doing," he told her and walked to the back of the shop.

"Ain't that Duke truck?" Tina asked as soon as La-La turned into the parking lot.

"Yep, he probaly in there pussy hunting."

"You better than me because I couldn't just let a nigga cheat on me."

La-La looked over at her best friend before getting out of the car. "That nigga got enough money to have any woman that he wants, but he sleep with me every night. You do the math."

Faces started frowning up as soon as La-La and Tina walk through the doors of Bayshun Hair and Nail Salon. La-La stopped to look around the room.

"You ain't gotta be quiet because you see me, do what you do."

Snooppy and her two friends, Dee and Shay, kept talking because they could care less about La-La.

"Dee, the nigga don't wanna do shit but fuck you and stick you in a house somewhere."

"He got it like that."

Snooppy was looking as if she didn't know who she was referring to. "That nigga got enough money to make you eat ya moma pussy. . . on the real. I'm just getting it while the getting is good."

"Ain't that his main thang?" Shay asked, pointing at La-La. "Her man fucking half of Monroe . . . ooh, don't she feel special."

Snooppy slapped high fives with Shay and Dee, falling over laughing. La-La wasn't paying them the least bit of attention, but Tina had heard every word. She was eavesdropping on everyone's conversation.

"You heard that bitch over there?"

"Nope, why, what she say?"

"She say Duke fucking half of Monroe, and you should feel special."

La-La dropped the hair magazine she was reading on the table and stood up. "Which one of them hoes you talking about?"

La-La wasn't big on fighting, but around the hood, it was a way of survival. She knew Duke had a lot of women, and he wasn't going to stop seeing them because of her. Yet La-La knew she was the only one who could say, "He bought me a half of a million dollar house and a V-12 Benz. She wasn't mad at the other females, because if he was giving, they were supposed to take it. On the same note, La-La refused to be disrespected. She took her earrings off and walked toward the hair dryers.

"What was you saying about Duke?"

Snooppy took a glance up but kept talking as though she didn't see La-La. "My shit gone be the bomb, and you know I'ma fuck some—"

La-La hit her in the mouth and didn't stop swinging. Snooppy tried to stand up, but the blows were raining down too hard and coming too fast.

"Hit that bitch, La-La . . . hit that hoe."

Duke looked up at the camera monitor on the wall. "They up there fighting," he said, looking at Shelby.

She shook her head. "I told you about coming to my shop pussy hunting. Now look . . . you need to go out there and take yo crazy-ass girlfriend home."

"I'm not going out there, Shelby. Boo, go help yo sister break that shit up."

Shelby was pissed to the third degree. She and Boo ran to the front of the salon and broke up the one-sided fight.

"I don't give a fuck who fucking who—you bitches better get the fuck out my shop, right now."

La-La broke free from the hold Boo had on her. "I don't know who you calling a bitch, but me and you can go too."

Boo tried to grab La-La, but she stepped back, holding her hands up. "I swear to God, if you touch me again, nigga, I'm going to the car to get my gun."

"Bitch, get out my—"

Tina sucker-punched Shelby in the mouth, and she stumbled back. La-La and Tina grabbed their purses and walked out the door.

* * *

"You gone have the whole neighborhood knocking on your door," Duke told Shawn, walking through her front door.

"Here, nigga, you just saying that because you want some."

He took a bite of the steaming crispy hot chicken. "I need you to open as many businesses as possible with the money you got stashed for me."

"You can lie to my moma all you want, but I know you back selling dope. In the last eighteen months, you done brought me every bit of five or six million dollars. Not counting the safe deposit boxes and what we done spent."

Duke grabbed another piece of chicken. "I quit hustling, big sis—"

"You making too much money to quit hustling, Duke. Look at this." She slid the marble countertop to the side, revealing a stash spot. "You drop this half a million dollars off yesterday. Shit Duke, you bringing me so much money that I'm running out of places to hide it."

He gave her a kiss on the cheek. "Come see, my new truck."

Shawn stuck her head out the door. "Ooh-wee, you gone have to let me get that one."

"Nope, but you can buy you and Aunt Roz something new if you want to."

"Who is that sitting in your truck waving at me?"

"La-La crazy ass."

Shawn waved back. "Bye . . . boy."

Chapter 12
The Gift

Miami, Florida, is a city that never sleeps, from the strip clubs to fancy restaurants, you can always find some excitement. This was the place Duke considered his second home. Whether it be business or pleasure, he was in Miami three times a month. Success was looming over his head as he punched in the code at the front gate of his estate. Over the past year, the game had truly blessed him. From sitting on Allen Street peddling rocks, to flipping two hundred birds a month, the game was definitely good.

The car came to a stop in front of an 11,000-square-foot, six-bedroom, twelve-bath-and-a-half, and an eight-car-garage palace.

"What rich muthafucka live here?" Tina asked, hopping out of the car.

"Me," Duke responded while grabbing the bags from the trunk.

La-La stood looking around. "This is a big-ass house, though."

"Shid, this a castle compared to my apartment."

Duke watched the women go upstairs, before punching in a code on the hidden wall keypad. A hydraulic jack came to life, raising a safe up out of the middle of the living room floor. He pressed down on the fingerprinting mechanism and heard the lock click. The money stack neatly inside the safe was a sign that his hard work was finally paying off. Dre had been charging him 9.5 a key, and Duke was buying no less than 200 at a time. Although, this time around, he was planning to buy enough dope to retire off of. The only problem was that Duke would need Dre to lower the price just a tad -bit. After cleaning out the safe, he two-way-paged Dre.

"La-La," he hollered, standing at the bottom of the stairs.

"Huh."

"You being nosy up there?"

She came down the steps. "We doing girl stuff."

"I'a be in the backyard if you need me, then."

"OK."

Becoming a hustler was a blessing in disguise. After years and years of struggling to make ends meet, he was finally out of the hood. After everything he had been through, Duke had the right to feel good about his success. His goal started out being a few hundred thousand dollars, but then life set in. Six months after his release, Duke had touched close to 10 million dollars. He said he would quit after 5 million more, but that was two years ago.

"Now that's a big-ass pool," La-La said, looking over his shoulder at the M-shaped pool.

"It might get bigger if you get in it."

"We sho can see," Tina and La-La both responded, making their way back in the house.

La-La stuck her head back out the door. "Someone knocking at the door . . . you want me to get it?"

"Nah, gone go put on that bathing suit. You already know I love to see you in a thong."

Duke grabbed the MP5 from the kitchen cabinet before walking over to the door. "Who is it?" he asked, putting his eye on the peephole.

"It's me."

Duke let the first garage door up, and Dre pulled the Maserati Quattroporte in. He put the two duffel bags in the trunk before hopping in the car.

"Another day, huh," Duke said, slamming the door.

"You know I do it."

Duke laughed because Dre always play'd the broke role, but he knew Dre had long money. He didn't show it, but the real estate, yachts, private planes, and exotic car lots spoke for themselves.

"So how's business?" Duke asked, letting his seat back to get comfortable.

"As usual, I guess . . . just bought out a Lamborghini dealership on the riverfront. You should stop by sometime."

"Man, I got a storage full of the cars you already done gave me. You got something new, though."

Dre smiled. "I got something special for you, this time."

"I'ma need a lower ticket, Dre."

Dre grabbed the Cuban cigar from the ashtray and took a long drag before responding.

"How many we talking?"

Duke hunched his shoulders. "About a half of a ton or so."

"Since it's you and I know the potential you have, how's five thousand a kilo?" He stubbed the cigar out in the ashtray. "But you will have to take another half a ton on cosignment for the regular price."

Dollar signs were bouncing before his eyes as he counted the figures in his head. Duke realized that he was about to be filthy rich; there was no turning back after this run. The deal of his life was stamped and sealed with a handshake.

"The three and a half mil in the trunk, plus the five million you picked up with the Suburban . . . my balance should be six mil, right."

Dre nodded his head in agreement. "Be at the car lot before daybreak, and don't be late."

He let Dre out and went back in the house. The mere thought of what had just taken place had him nervous. From where he was standing, Duke could see La-La and Tina having a water fight in the pool. Tina saw him watching and got out of the pool to get her a drink. Duke had to look down at the blunt he was rolling to keep his eyes off of Tina's plump ass. La-La walked up, pulling her hair back into a pony tail.

"Come on, get in, baby," she said, giving him a seductive look.

"I'm hungry."

"What's in the kitchen to cook, then?"

"Everything you can think of," he responded, pulling her down on his lap.

She stuck her hand in his pants, stroking him up and down. "Can I eat some of this?"

"You nasty as hell."

Tina got up from the bar to go in the house. The extra step in her walk made her ass shake out of control.

"What are you looking at?" La-La asked, looking in his eyes.

"Nothing."

Duke tried not to look at Tina, but her pussy-print was fatter than a camel's foot. He thought about asking La-La for a threesome but didn't want to break her heart. It was bad enough that he didn't let her give him head because he didn't want to taste his own dick whenever they kissed. It really didn't matter, though, because he knew Tina would open the door before long. Tina helped La-La fry catfish, shrimp, and curly fries in record time. Duke took his plate and sat out on the back dock. La-La took a shower to wash the chlorine off her body and went out on the dock to sit with Duke.

"Now I see why you always come to Miami."

He looked back over his shoulder and saw La-La standing behind his chair. "I love the weather, but it's mostly business for me. Don't get me wrong, though . . . night life here is off the chain."

"So what's on your mind?"

"The same thing as yesterday."

La-La sat down on his lap. "You know I got you."

"I know that, but what's up with ya, girl. You can't drive both vehicles back home."

"Just let me take care of Tina, OK. Oh yea, please, and I do mean this, Duke. Do not have sex with her. I know how you is, and I know my girl," she told him with a stern look on her face.

He gave La-La a kiss on the cheek and neck. "Make me happy, then."

*   *   *

Baby and BG rushed Conrad as soon as he unlocked the front door of his condo. Tonet heard the dogs barking and came to see what was going on.

"Hey, stranger," she said, watching him play with the dogs.

Hearing her sweet voice always put a smile on his face. Out of all the women he came across, Conrad could honestly say that she was one of the good ones.

"I got a few problems . . . can I get some counseling or something?"

"It all depends, because you know how you is. Sometimes I think you should be doing my job."

He knew she was unhappy about his drug dealings, and Tonet had every right to be. Conrad was supposed to have retired a million dollars ago. The way he was raised and the way she was raised was the reason for that. Conrad grew up in the projects, or the hood, as most people tend to call it. Tonet, on the other hand, was raised by her rich parents, who spoiled her rotten as an only child. After graduating from West Monroe High School, with honors, she attended Monroe Louisiana University to stay close to home. Bookwise, she was a straight A student; but as far as the streets, Tonet was as dumb as a box of rocks. When Tonet began her first semester, Conrad was a regular on campus. He was well known for selling any drug that would turn a profit. Tonet was cheerleader captain, and didn't know Conrad or what he did for a living. Conrad saw her one night after a homecoming game and made cat calls to get her attention, but Tonet kept walking. He ran up behind her and grabbed hold of her arm.

"Don't be acting funny, Ms. Cheerleader Captain."

"You don't have to hold my arm . . . I'm not going to run away," she said, looking down at his hand.

Conrad let go of her arm and almost spat in her face. "You rich hoes drive the Benz yo people bought you, act like yo shit don't stink. Yet the minute a white boy holla at you, you go head over heels."

"You don't even know—" she managed to say before being cut off.

"Don't even waste yo breath, and I'm sorry I wasted mine."

Conrad walked off and didn't look back. From that day forward, Tonet would stare at him whenever she saw Conrad but was too scared to say something. It wasn't hard to spot him: the Gucci, Fendi, and Iceberg that he wore made him stand out from the other students. While they were struggling to make ends meet with part-time jobs, Conrad was clocking ten grand a night. He and Diron were leaving the campus late one night, and a white girl flagged them down. Before he could get the window all the way down, she was asking him questions.

"You Conrad, huh?"

"You know her?" he asked, looking over at Diron.

"Why the fuck you gone ask me if I know her? She ask for you, nigga."

He opened the car door and got out to get a better look at her.

"Who told you my name?" he asked, looking at her breast rather than her face.

"You need to quit being so ugly to my friend, she really likes you."

"Look, I don't have time for whatever type of game you trying to play. You don't know me, and I don't know you or your friend. Better yet, leave me the fuck alone before I get mad."

She took a few steps back before responding. "You do know Tonet . . . she's the cheerleader captain."

Duke couldn't believe that Tonet had sent her geeky white girlfriend to confront him. He had just seen her earlier that day, and she hadn't said a word to him.

"Where she at now, then?"

"She in the dorm studying for midterm exams. If you want, you can use my key, and I'll stay here with him," she said, smiling at Diron.

He took the key and crept over to the women's dormitory. It didn't really matter to him if he got caught, because he was a student. Conrad unlocked the room door and locked it back after entering. For a moment, he wondered why he was there and thought about leaving. Yet when he heard the running water and singing, he knew he had come to the right place. Conrad sat on the edge of the desk and saw six 700-page books under a night light. With all those pages to read, he could only imagine what her major was. Tonet didn't see him when she came out of the bathroom and sat on the bed.

"Dam girl, I ain't know you was that dam fine," he said, walking toward her.

Tonet froze at the sound of his voice and resembled a deer caught in a pair of headlights. Conrad stepped between Tonet's legs and pushed her down on the bed.

"Yo white friend said you wanted to see me," he told her, holding up the room key.

Tonet nodded her head, but she didn't speak. Conrad rubbed the wet spot between her thighs, and Tonet's body began to relax.

"No, I can't . . . I mean, we can't. My moma told me not to have sex until I graduate from college and get married."

"You saying you a virgin?" he asked, getting excited.

"Uh-huh," she responded shyly.

The word *virgin* was music to his ears. Every man in the world has had a fantasy about breaking some young woman's virginity. Tonet's mom was going to have to be mad at Conrad because he wasn't passing up an opportunity like this. His boxers and pants fell down to his ankles, and Tonet almost passed out. She sat up straight, but Conrad lay on top of her, forcing her to lie back down on the bed.

"Don't do this to me, Conrad, please. I can't . . . Don't," she screamed as he entered her.

Conrad penetrated her with force, and she screamed loud enough for God to hear it. He put her legs on his shoulders and pulled her to him by her shoulders. Tonet drew blood from his back as he pounded in and out of her. He flipped Tonet over, pounding her until she began to cry. Conrad knew she was in pain, but her screams excited him more and more.

A month later, he made a stop by her room and found Tonet in tears sitting on the bed.

"Calm down and tell me, what's wrong?" he told her, wiping the tears from her eyes.

"I'm . . . I'm pregnant . . . Conrad. My moma not gonna pay for my tuition if I have a baby."

She buried her head in his chest and cried her heart out. For the first time, Conrad was stunned. He didn't know what to say. The thought of her killing his first child made Conrad sick to the stomach. He got angry and pushed Tonet off his lap.

"You gone kill my baby?"

Conrad knew that this was what she was thinking when she didn't look up at him.

"I don't have a choice," she stated in a matter-of-fact way.

"Oh, now you don't have a choice. You come hunt me down for dick by choice, yet, the minute you get pregnant, you don't have a choice. What type of fucking shit is that."

Tonet tried to put her arms around him, but Conrad pushed her away.

"Don't do me like this . . . I'm sorry." She wiped the tears away that were falling from her eyes. "I know I'm being selfish, but this is my only way out. I can't even—"

Conrad shot her a look that could kill.

"I can't stop you from doing what you have your mind made up to do. Choosing a career over our child is something you gonna have to live with." He didn't know he was crying until the tears began to roll down his neck. "I'ma give you the money and let you make the choice. And as of today, you better not call your moms and ask her for nothing, so you better have a job in two weeks, or we through."

He dropped ten 100-dollar bills on the bed and stumbled out of the door. This was five years ago. Conrad and Tonet would never forget that day. She rubbed the back of his head before walking around the chair to sit in his lap.

"I need you to set up my lick."

She laid her head on his chest and looked in his eyes. "Just tell me who you want and what I need to do to get him."

Tonet was so innocent that Conrad didn't like involving her in his illegal dealings. Yet she was the only female he trusted outside of Shawn and Roz. Then with her owning her own YMCA, it put her in a bad position. But Conrad could care less about that at the moment—he needed what he needed, and that was the end of that.

"We can go over the details when I pick you up for lunch."

The puppy look that she was giving him meant that Tonet wanted something. It was strange, but he knew her better than she knew herself.

"How much is it gonna cost me?"

"It's ladies' night tonight . . . please."

"Which club?"

She gave him a soft kiss on the lips. "Me and Mea gone go to Club Shakers."

Conrad smiled. "Yo can go, but don't make this no habit."

"Coach yo hoes, I know my position," she stated, standing up to leave.

*   *   *

Chapter 13
The Curse

Liz Claiborne, Michael Kors, Gucci, Prada, BCBG, Cristian Dior, and Louis Vuitton—*tired* wasn't the word. La-La and Tina were walking Duke in and out of stores. La-La would search the whole store for an hour and find out they didn't have anything she wanted. La-La saw the look on Duke's face and headed for the exit.

"We going home?" she asked with a hint of sarcasm.

"Nope, I got a surprise for you."

Tina and the shopping bags left in a taxi, while Duke took La-La to his favorite eatery in Miami. They walked into the restaurant at Minary and were greeted by a petty white waitress.

"Welcome to River West, how may I be of service to you?"

"Do you have an opening on the back patio?" Duke asked with a big smile on his face.

She rolled her eyes at La-La. "Would you take a booth?"

La-La smacked the taste out of her mouth before Duke realized what happened. The waitress dropped the clipboard and followed it to the floor. The manager saw the commotion up front and rushed over to see what was going on.

"Excuse me, but are we having a problem?"

La-La pulled Duke away. "I don't wanna eat here." She pointed to the waitress. "Hoes like that don't know how to treat someone like me."

Another write-up would probably cost him his job, so the manager didn't need any more problems.

"Kera, you're fired," he told the waitress, who was still on the floor holding her face. He looked back at La-La with a smile on his face. "I'm sorry for the inconvenience, and I would love to give you a meal of your choice, on the house."

"Well, get us a spot on the patio," La-La demanded.

"Sure thing . . . Follow me right this way."

Once they were seated in a secluded area on the patio, the manager hurried off to fulfill their orders.

"I thought they say money change people. You still getto as hell, woman," he told her, laughing.

"She better be thanking the Lord that I was with you and not Tina."

"Calm yo crazy ass down and fix your face. We gone get that new house when we—"

"Quit buying me all of this material shit, Duke. It can't take the place of you being gone all the time."

"What, you saying you don't want it."

She put her hands over his. "That's not what I'm saying. I just don't want you to think that I want you for your money."

"See, you know the right shit to say, and that's why I love you. The thing is . . ."

The manager wheeled a cart up to the side of their table. "Enjoy your meal, and call me if you need anything else."

La-La was staring at Duke; she wasn't paying the manager any attention.

"The thing is what?" she asked with an attitude.

"I don't want you to think that we are losing touch just because things are changing. It's just that I've been so focused on coming up with the money for this shipment."

She nodded her head, letting him know that she understood. Duke took her to the beach once they finished with their meal. They took off their shoes and chased one another until they were out of breath. He couldn't remember the last time that he had had so much fun doing the simple things in life. The more time that he spent with La-La, the more that he realized love was something that money couldn't buy.

"My feet ain't plan on all this walking, baby girl. Come on over here and take seat."

Duke sat down, and La-La sat between his legs.

"The water is so clear you can see straight to the bottom. We gone have to get us a big fish tank with some tropical fish in it. If that's fine with you."

Duke made a mental note to buy her a big fish tank, with plenty of tropical fish.

"Look over there," he said, pointing out in the water.

La-La pulled out her phone to snap some pictures of the dolphins.

"You see how they stick together."

"Yep," she said, still snapping pictures.

"I wish I could get my people to stick together, like that."

"You can," she responded before being cut off with a kiss.

Duke slid his hand under her skirt and slid her G-string down to her knees. La-La finished taking them off and gave them to him.

"Is this what you want?" she asked, twirling them on her index finger.

He grabbed the panties and stuck them in his pocket. "This ain't all I want, though."

La-La felt like a real woman. No words could explain the way he kissed and touched the most sensitive parts of her body. The waves crashed into the bank as cries and moans began to escape her lips. Duke put it on La-La so strong she went straight to sleep when they made it home. He was tired himself, but he had other things on his mind. Tina was in the living room watching TV when he came back downstairs.

"What's good?" he asked, sitting on the sofa beside her.

"I was on my way to sleep."

Duke grabbed the remote and flipped the TV to the Playboy station.

"I know you ain't gone leave it on this," she said, sitting up.

"Let me find out if watching somebody else fuck bring the freak out of you."

She looked in his eyes. "Between me and you, how should I say it. I see the way you was looking at—"

"Look," Duke said, cutting her off, pointing at the TV. "He fucking the shit out that hoe."

"Are you listening to me?"

"Yea, I'm listening to you. Offer me some pussy."

Tina didn't have to admit it, because the look on her face said it all. Duke knew she was waiting for him to come back downstairs. He stood between her legs and spread them as wide as they would go. He reached down to pull her panties off, and his hand touched bare skin. Tina had been listening to Duke and La-La have sex early that day. The moaning and bed clapping had her aroused and kept her panties moist all day. Duke bent over the sofa and dug in as deep as he could. Tina got used to that position, and he sat her up straight on the sofa with her legs on his shoulders. Duke was pounding her so hard in that position that he had to put his hand over her mouth to muffle her cries. Tina was shaking and breathing hard. Before long, Duke knew his mission was accomplished.

"Boy"—she wiped the sweat from her forehead—"now I see why La-La in love with you. Boy, you be working that thang."

He stood up and put his boxers back on. "Look out for me, and I'a give you some dick every day."

"I need more than dick because dick can't pay my bills."

"I gave you ten grand earlier, and I'ma give you fifteen grand when we make it back to Monroe. If you don't want that, I can take you to the airport and send you home right now."

She began to straighten up the living room. "I'ma take that, but you have to do better next time. For now, I'm not dumb, and you not dealing with crumbs."

"Yea, all right . . . whatever."

La-La was still sleep when he slid back in bed. After smoking a blunt of hydro, he put pipe on her every way but the wrong way.

*　　*　　*　　*　　*

Tonet pulled into the parking lot of Club Shakers and valet-parked the Benz. She glanced from right to left, then did an about-face. She had to make sure everyone saw the baddest bitch enter the building.

The hood on her waist-length chinchilla covered head as she brushed imaginary dirt from the bejeweled Jimmy Choo stilettos on her feet. With the Roberto Cavalli one-piece wrap skirt fitting like a glove, she knew that she was the shit.

"Somebody gone snipe yo crazy ass if you don't come on," Mea said, pulling her by the arm.

"They just mad that they momas don't look this good," she stated with a smile.

The bouncer gave Mea her tag but put Tonet's around his neck. "I'ma have to pat-search you."

"Pat-search this." She pulled a crispy one-hundred-dollar bill from her handbag and held it in the air.

He took the money, and she snatched the tag out of his hand. An escort took them to their booth and passed their orders off to their waitress. Out of the four VIP rooms, she ended up in the right one; her mark was on the other side of the room having a ball. Today was definitely her lucky day.

"Watch me work, MeMe," she said, standing to her feet.

"Go head wit yo slick ass."

Tonet sashayed over to the DJ's booth and leaned over the banister. "Play three songs for me, and I'ma give you a C-note for every song you play."

The DJ figured she was high or drunk—either way, he was happy.

"I would of did it for you for free, but I can't turn down no bread. What songs you want to hear?"

"Play 'Goodies,' 'Slow Motion,' and 'Like Glue' back to back."

Tonet downed two shots of vodka at the bar and made her way to the dance floor. The DJ dropped "Goodies," and she went to work. Her body was moving with the beat so good that men and women were gawking. Her years of running track and practicing cheers were finally paying off. Groups of men were beginning to surround the dance floor. Every eye in the club was trying to get a peep at the red bone with an ass that jiggled like Jell-O. Tonet saw their reactions through the mirrors around the dance floor and shook her ass harder. The first two songs went by with ease, and she put the icing on the cake with 'Like Glue.' The way she moved her hips and ass, barely moving her legs, had everyone going crazy.

"I thought them hoes was gone try to strangle me," she said, taking a seat beside Mea.

"Shid, them niggas look like they was gone eat you up," she responded, laughing.

The waitress walked up with a tray full of drinks and set them down on the table.

"You got a lot of fans, home girl. Eight different niggas sent you drinks."

She handed the waitress a fifty-dollar bill. "That's cool and all, but go pour that shit out."

She gave Tonet a bewildered look but knew that she meant what she was saying. "Tell them niggas I said that I can buy myself a drink. If they really want my attention, tell them to send it by the bottle."

"Can I buy you a bottle, then?" a light-skinned young dude asked, stopping in front of her.

"I'm cool. Meme, you want a bottle?"

Mea wanted to laugh, but she held it in. "Why not?"

He gave Tonet a twisted look before walking off. Conrad came out of nowhere with two bottles of Louis XIII. Mea didn't know who he was, and Tonet didn't bother to inform her.

"You got these niggas drooling over you, baby girl."

She tapped the seat beside her. "Come on, sit down and have a drink."

"Are we still on?"

"Is money green?"

Conrad smiled. "I'ma catch you another time, then."

"Who was that?" Mea ask when Conrad walked away.

"Some nigga who been stalking me."

Tonet looked across the room and saw AP looking as drunk as a skunk. It was looking easier than she thought it would be. Pussy and alcohol were more powerful than most people knew. The waitress walked up, smiling, with two glasses and two bottles of Cristal in hand.

"The dude who sent these said you have a nice outfit on."

Tonet looked at who the waitress said sent the bottle and saw that her plan was starting to come together. She stuck three more hundreds in the pocket of the waitress's apron and whispered in her ear, "Tell dude meet me at the valet box in five minutes."

"OK," she replied, walking away. She dropped the valet ticket on the table. "Take my car to your house, and I'ma call you in the morning."

"Gone get some dick for a change."

Tonet saw AP walking out the exit door and took that as her cue.

"I just hooked a fish, Meme."

*   *   *

Cars zoomed by beneath the Renwick Street walkover bridge. Shagg and Will were standing guard at opposite ends of the bridge. On top of the bridge, Hotboy, Conrad, and Boo were beating blood out of Tocky. Before Mann was killed, Tocky and his crew were working for him. The word got around that Mann was dead, and Tocky took over the operation, which spread over 70 percent of the east side of Monroe. Conrad saw him at the club and made Tocky an offer. He felt offended and treated Conrad like a two-dollar whore on the fast track. Conrad felt played, and they kidnapped Tocky after he left the club.

"You gone give me what I want, or some lucky driver gone think it's raining bodies," Conrad said, leaning over the rail talking to Tocky.

"I can, man . . . that's all—"

"Drop him."

They leaned Tocky farther over the rail, and he began to cry.

"Please . . . Conrad, man . . . please."

"This my last time asking."

"OK. . . OK . . . Please, Conrad . . . please, don't kill me. The money and dope over my moma crib on Church Street."

Conrad tapped Hotboy and Boo on the shoulder, and they lifted Tocky back over the rail.

"Get yo bitch ass up and . . . let's get that from yo mammy's crib."

*   *   *   *

Tonet sat back on the black Italian leather sofa with her legs crossed.

"Why you looking at me like that?"

He licked his lips. "I could just eat you up . . . dam, you'sa fine, muthafucca."

She slapped his hand away as soon as he put it on her leg. AP figured that a little more liquor might loosen her up.

"You want something to drink?"

"Yea, bring me the strongest drink you got."

AP stood to his feet and wobbled toward the kitchen. He was so drunk that he had to use the wall for support. She made her move as soon as he turned his back. Tonet pulled the Visine from her handbag and squeezed the whole bottle in his glass. Conrad told her that it would only take a few drops, but she figured that there wasn't much of a difference. AP came back with her drink and plopped down on the couch beside her. The first thing that he did was down the rest of his drink sitting on the table. *Fool*, she said to herself. *You never leave your drink unattended and drink it when you come back.*

"Why you wanted to come to my crib?" AP asked, staring up at the ceiling.

"To be honest, you wouldn't understand. Let's go in yo room and talk."

AP was already undressing before they were in the bedroom. She unsnapped the skirt and stood in the doorway wearing only a hot-pink thong. She pushed AP down on the bed and began to kiss his stomach.

"Stay right here while I go freshen up."

He tried to grab her by the arm when she reached down to pick up her handbag, but she pushed him back on the bed.

"You look and feel just right to me. Come on get back in the bed."

"Let me shower, and I'ma come suck the skin off of that dick."

AP's face lit up like Times Square on Christmas Eve. Nothing turns a man on more than mentioning sucking his dick. She learned that from being around Conrad.

"Let me shower with you, then," he said, holding his erect penis.

She wanted to laugh at how stupid he sounded. "Just stay right here, and I'ma dim the lights."

She locked the bathroom door and let out a nervous burst of laughter. After turning the shower on and lighting a blunt to calm her nerves, she called Conrad."

"I got him . . ."

"Where you at?"

"In the new condos in West Monroe. Room 355 . . . de left end of the third floor."

"I'm on the way."

She sat in the bathroom for ten more minutes before coming out. She was silently praying that AP was out cold when she opened the bathroom door. She gathered up her clothing before going in the living to unlock the door. AP didn't have the slightest idea what he was in for, but he was most definitely about to find out.

"He in the bedroom sleep. I didn't fu—" she informed Conrad before he cut her off.

"Drive my car home, and I'a be there soon."

Conrad locked the door and gave Shagg a pair of latex gloves to put on.

"Pour the bleach on everything, and whatever you do, don't take those gloves off. Oh yea, bring me some trash bags when you finish in here."

Conrad cuffed AP's legs to his arms and put duct tape over his mouth. He cut the cord off the TV and tied knots in it. When the cord came down on his naked body, AP bucked like a wild horse. Conrad beat him with the cord until blood was everywhere.

"Where the money and dope at?" he asked, standing over AP with the cord raised in the air.

"UMM . . . UMM . . . UMM . . . UMM," he cried out.

"Don't cry," Conrad teased, laughing.

Shagg burst out laughing when he walked through the bedroom door.

"You beating this nigga and ain't tell me."

Shagg grabbed the lamp off the nightstand and beat AP so bad that Conrad thought he was dead. Shagg snatched the duct tape off his mouth.

"Where the shit at?" he asked, twirling the lamp in his hand.

"It's in the closet—just take it and leave."

Shagg hit him with the lamp. "Shut up."

Conrad went through the shoeboxes in the closet and found the money. He dumped the money in a trash bag and threw the bag to Shagg.

"I don't see the dope," he said, looking over his shoulder.

Shagg put the Desert Eagle to AP's head, and AP almost had a heart attack.

"I'ma tell you . . . I'ma tell you, please don't kill me."

"Start talking, nigga," Conrad demanded.

"It's hidden under the bed in the compartment."

Conrad dropped down to his knees and snatched one of the boards off the side of the bed. He couldn't believe how many kilos were under the bed.

"Give me some bags."

He put 10 kilos in four different bags and 5 kilos in the fifth one. The five keys that were left, Conrad broke them up all over the room. Shagg was opening the door when he realized that Conrad wasn't behind him.

"What is you doing, let's go," Shagg told him, peeping out in the hallway.

"Take the shit and I'ma see you in a li'l while."

"Man . . ."

"I said go . . . dam."

Shagg left out the apartment through the back door, and Conrad went back in the bedroom. AP began to shake when he saw Conrad standing over him.

"Ask God to forgive you for all the dope you done sold."

"Don't kill—" he managed to say before being cut off.

Conrad put a plastic bag over his head and pulled on it as tight as he could.

"Pray. You bitch . . . I said pray," he spat out, feeling AP's body growing limp.

Chapter 14
Dime a Dozen

A black 600 Benz with 5 percent tint on the window pulled into Will's driveway and sat there.

"Girl, who is that?" Mona asked, straining to see who was behind the tint.

Trina shifted in the plastic chair. "That's the nigga that will be fucking with. They say he the nigga with all the money."

"An he rolling like that?"

Lanny was tiring of this conversation already. "That's the same nigga who got all these hoes running around here like a chicken with their heads cut off."

Mona turned to the usually quiet Lanny. "How you know who he is?"

"He fronting everybody and they moma dope around here, who don't know the nigga?"

A cloud of smoke gushed out of the Benz as Duke slid out from behind the wheel.

"Will in there?" he asked, walking up to the porch.

"Nope, he in the back alleyway."

Mona tapped the back of Trina's chair. "Introduce us," she whispered.

"My bad. Duke, these are my best friends."

"That's Mona, and this is Lanny."

Duke looked over the two females sitting with Trina. "What's up?" He turned back to Trina. "If you don't mind, Trina, go get Will for me."

Without saying another word, Trina jumped from the porch and disappeared around the side of the house.

"You can come sit with us. But I can't promise not to bite," Mona informed him, seductively licking her lips.

Duke was about to give her a sarcastic remark, but Trina and Will walked up. Will went in the house and came back out with four foot locker bags.

"Where she from?" Duke asked as soon as Will got in the car.

"Who?" Will asked, looking around.

Duke pointed up on the porch, and Will knew exactly who he was talking about.

"Oh, you talking about Mona. Shid . . . I heard"—Will lit the blunt he had been holding—"she got that 'snap back and blow ya mind' head game."

"Sit them bags on the floorboard in the back. I'ma call you in a li'l while to tell you where to meet me at."

Will nodded his head before exiting the car. Duke waved his hand out the window to get Mona's attention. She gave Trina and Lanny a big Kool-Aid smile as Mona strutted over to the Benz.

"Get in and let's take a ride."

Mona stuck her tongue out at Lanny and Trina. "I'a be back."

"Let's bet she'a be back in about thirty minutes," Lanny inquired, holding her hand out.

"How you know how long she gone be gone?"

"I said let's bet," she said, still holding out her hand.

Duke cracked the sunroof and backed out of the driveway. As the blunt smoke filled his lungs, Duke was trying to make up his mind. Did he want to sample her mouth or her ass? Remembering how she licked her lips, he decided on her head game—plus, he had some important stops to make, so he was pressed for time. He boldly unzipped his pants and let his manhood stand up through the opening in his boxers.

"Let's try not to bite," he told her, adjusting his seat.

Mona rub the fuck-me red lipstick off her lips with the back of her hand.

The things women do for men with money. Duke felt like a king as Mona went to work on him. The way she was giving him deep throat had to be illegal. Mona wasn't new to giving head game; she was a pro. Duke's foot was so heavy on the pedal that he ran two stop signs before he could stop the car. Once her deed was done, Duke dropped Mona back off and drove to his townhouse. Smoke was everywhere when he turned the corner. He thought the sun had fallen from the sky and landed on his house. His neighbors were pointing at his car when he drove up.

"Why the fuck you standing around . . . put this shit out," he spat out at the firefighters standing around.

"Are you Kewhan Wright?" one of the firefighters asked, taking a step toward Duke.

"Why . . . what the fuck that got to do with my house burning down?"

He flashed a badge. "I'm FBI, and you're under arrest, smartass."

"Get the fuck off me," Duke screamed, pushing him back. "I don't give a fuck who you is, nigga. If my house burn down, you gonna be working in Iraq somewhere."

Seven more agents dressed up like firefighters rushed Duke and slammed him facefirst to the concrete.

"Cuff him and search that," the agent said, pointing at the Benz.

*   *   *

A stack of manila folders was slammed down on the table in front of Duke. Agent Rylon sat back in his chair across from Duke with his legs crossed.

"We have reason to believe that you are involved in these murders," he told Duke, tapping the stack of folders.

"I haven't done shit, and I don't know shit."

Agent Rylon flipped the top folder open.

"Let's see, where were you August the nineteenth?"

"Like I said, I don't—" Duke responded before being cut off.

"According to a statement given by Elmore Roger and Leroy Jenkins, I hear you're planning a takeover."

Duke sat back in the chair and didn't say a word. He was far too smart to incriminate himself in any form or fashion. The agent realized he wasn't playing with a rookie and slammed the folder shut.

"Two weeks after, you force your way inside." He reopened the top folder before continuing, "Club ballers and poke your uncle's eye out, Anthony Price, a.k.a. AP is found dead in his condo. He was robbed and smothered with a plastic bag."

Agent Rylon leaned over the table and tossed some pictures in Duke's face.

"Look at it . . . look at it—that's what you're responsible for."

Duke glanced down at the pictures, and his facial expression didn't change. He politely picked the pictures up from the floor and sat them on the table.

"Are you finished?" he asked, looking down at the Cartier watch on his wrist.

Agent Rylon had a look on his face like he wanted to jump across the table and strangle Duke. "I'm just beginning," he replied, standing to his feet.

"Well, you can tell the rest of that shit to my lawyer."

Without another word, Duke was escorted back to his dorm by a CO. As soon as he walked through the door, Duke got in line to use the phone. It was still early, so he was hoping to catch La-La. He'd been calling her all morning but couldn't reach her.

"Hello."

"Where the fuck you at? I been calling you all morning."

"I been over Roz house, and you know we get a bad cell phone reception over here."

Duke gave the dude behind him waiting to use the phone a cold stare. He tried to play it off, but Duke knew he was eavesdropping on his conversation.

"Somebody burned up the townhouse and my Impala. The feds showed up dress like firefighters and locked me up." He put his hand over the phone. "A half a mil got burned up in my Impala, and they took another half a mil when they picked me up. Hold on . . . say, nigga, get the fuck out my—"

"Baby, who is you talking to," she asked, cutting him off.

"I'm not talking to you, just listen."

"OK, I'm listening."

"Get in touch with Shawn and have her call the lawyer I told her about."

"You don't want me to get some money out of my safe deposit box to bond you out."

"Just do what I said do, bye."

He hung up the phone before she could respond and went to his cell. It was strange to see how people act when they know someone has money. CO and inmates were kissing Duke's ass with hopes of getting a blessing. He tried not to be rude, but he had a lot on his mind. Duke was just getting into a deep sleep when someone tapped the end of his bunk.

"You've been released," a female voice informed Duke as he sat up.

He wiped the sleep out of his eyes. "What time is it?"

"Around 4:00 a.m."

Duke walked out of the Federal Plaza, once again a free man. He was mad and scared at the same time. Mad at the fact that he'd sat in a cell all day and scared because he was sitting on enough dope to send everyone he knew to jail.

"You need a lift."

Duke looked through the passenger window of the money-green 750 that pulled up in front of him.

"I ain't know you get up this early," he stated, opening the car door.

"Don't play. I got the call from your sister and been on it since."

For Mrs. Washington to be in her late forties, she was giving most twenty-one-year-old women hell. With long blonde hair falling to the small of her back and piercing emerald-green eyes, she was very attractive. Being that Mrs. Washington was a supermodel in her younger days and her ass was that of a black woman's, Duke was drawn to her.

"Did my sister send me them clothes I ask for?" he asked, reclining his seat back.

"They in the trunk, you know."

"Why is the feds riding me like this," he asked, cutting her off.

"If you quit cutting me off, I can explain to you." She made a left turn off the main road and turned into a parking lot connected to the pier. "They didn't have a search warrant for your car, nor a warrant for your arrest. I have a check for a quarter of a million dollars, minus my commission. It's for the house and the car that they let burn to the ground," she told him with a smile.

"What about the money that was in my Benz?"

"Oh yea, don't ever ride around with that type of money on you."

"I was picking up."

"Don't even worry about it because they're turning it over to Shawn," she told him while pushing a string of blonde hair out of her face.

"So how much do I owe you for that?"

"You owe me breakfast, lunch, dinner, and a nightcap on my yacht," she informed him, pointing to the houseboat docked at the pier.

"Oh, so you blackballing me now."

She put her hand on his leg. "I guess so."

*   *   *   *

Huge snowflakes were falling nonstop as Shagg drove Duke to Club Beemers. Beemers was labeled the hood club, but Duke loved the hood, because the hood was making him rich. Shagg wore a pink-and-blue Louis Vuitton outfit with custom-made timberlands. Duke, on the other hand, wore gator from head to toe, a full-length chinchilla fur, and enough ice to put two ice cubes inside of every cup inside of the club. Every way he turned, someone was asking him to take a picture. Duke knew that it was harmless, but he couldn't give the feds a chance to get a picture of him from the club.

Club Beemers was jam-packed, and the line was still wrapped around the building. A group of females ran Duke over and knocked his Cartier shades to the floor as he was coming out of the restroom.

"Dam, you ain't gone, at least say excuse me." She followed his eyes to the shades under her foot. "What, you thank a bitch can't pay for them weak-ass shades?"

"Don't trip, buy me a drink and we'a call it even."

"Slow down, playboy. I'm Shorty, and you are?"

"Duke, the one and only."

Shorty felt like she was looking at the man of her dreams. "Oh, you the nigga everybody be talking about."

"I know they talk bad about me because they talk bad about Jesus."

Shorty snatched one of the phones off of his hip before he could protest. She was about to store her number in it, but she saw that he had three more phones.

"You got four cell phones . . . business must be good. I mean, what do you do for a living?"

"I scout, buy, market, and resell."

Shorty put the phone in her handbag. "You might as well tell me what the number is because I'm keeping this phone."

"How I know you ain't just like these other women. I meet a hundred different women every day, this is nothing new to me. Oh yea, that phone is voice activated."

She didn't know what to say. "I can't do nothing but show you that I'm different. Better yet, I'm about to go tell my home gurl that I'm leaving with you."

Shorty left without another word, and Duke went back over to the table where Shagg was waiting on him.

"Dam, what, these hoes tryna kidnap you or something?"

"You know how it is."

It was after 3:00 a.m., and the club was slowly starting to wind down. Duke didn't see Shorty, so they made their exit before traffic got too bad. Shagg found an opening in the traffic and pulled in behind a truck. Duke grabbed the pistol off the floorboard when he saw a dark shadow hovering over his window.

"I know you not trying to leave me."

Shorty got in the back seat, and so did Duke.

"I can have him drop you off at home, or you can ride wit me to go get my car."

Shagg looked through the rearview mirror. "Cuzz, you can keep my car and just drop me off at the spot. You just gotta wash my shit before you bring it back, though."

"Boy, you know dam well that I ain't washing no car. Just drop me off at Roz crib, and I can get my car."

Shagg drove down Allen Avenue, and they saw India sitting outside. She saw Shorty sitting in the back with Duke. And her smile quickly turned into a frown. Although she had a man, she and Duke would still creep around from time to time. So seeing him with another woman did rub her the wrong way.

"Shagg, can you take me to work?" she asked, leaning in the window.

Shagg looked back and saw Duke shrugging his shoulders. "Come on."

"You want us to drop you off at home?" he asked Shorty while sliding his hand under her skirt.

"I'm all right . . . with yo slick ass."

"India, this is Shorty, and, Shorty, this is India.

"Hi."

"Hey!" Shorty shot back.

Shagg got on the highway, and Duke lit up a blunt. As soon as he passed the blunt to the front seat, he and Shorty were all over each other. He put two fingers inside of her while Shorty ran her tongue up and down his neck. Duke realized that they had been on the highway for a long time. It usually wouldn't have mattered, but he was ready to get Shorty home and break her off. The sign that they passed told him why they had been ridin' so long.

"Cuzz, where the fuck is you going?"

"North Monroe."

"You supposed to be on Highway 165 going north, not I-20 going north. Turn this bitch around at the next exit, cuzz.

Shagg drove for another fifteen miles, and instead of turning around, he made a right turn down a road leading to nowhere. Shagg fell asleep behind the wheel, and the car was heading for a ditch. India grabbed the steering wheel; Shagg woke up and snatched the wheel back from her. The car did a 360 spin, hit a trench, and slid sideways. Everyone started screaming because they were heading straight for a telegram pole.

"Turn the wheel . . . turn the fucking wheel!" Duke screamed, grabbing the headrest of Shagg's seat.

Shagg turned into the skid, and the car bounce, landing in the grass. The back bumper was completely torn off, and so was part of the front bumper.

"I can only imagine a week in yo life," Shorty said, looking at Duke. "We just met, and already 'bout to get me killed."

"India was tripping, man. She just grabbed the dam steering wheel. Cuzz, you know I wasn't sleep."

Shagg was trying his best to explain, but Duke knew his cousin better than anybody. The gas hand was sitting on E, and the road they were riding down was now a dead end. Duke was so mad that he almost slapped Shagg across the back of his head. Instead of putting his hands on him, he made Shagg pull over and got behind the wheel himself. As soon as he pulled back onto the road, Duke saw a police car in his rearview mirror. He pulled back onto the shoulder of the road and opened the door to get out.

"What the fuck is you doing?" Shagg asked, looking crazy.

"What the fuck you think I'm doing? We need help."

The police car was about to pass them by, but Duke stuck out his hand and flagged the car to stop.

"Excuse me, sir," Duke said when the window came down, "we are lost and about to run out of gas. Would you please direct me to the nearest gas station?"

"You go up three red lights and make a right. Follow that road, and the store will be on your left."

"Thank you, sir," Duke said, opening the car door.

"No problem."

Fifteen minutes later, they were gassed up and driving through Monroe. The car was noticeably quiet, with the close encounter still fresh on their minds.

Duke tapped India on her shoulder. "I think you done lost your job."

"I'm not even thinking about that job. I'm really just thanking God that I'm still alive."

He pulled seven crispy C-notes out of his pocket; Shorty was watching his every move.

"Here, this is a week up front. You can call my sister when you get home, and she will give you a job. Just tell her I sent you."

"Thank you."

"You ain't gotta thank me . . . don't steal from me."

They locked eyes through the rearview mirror. India knew that he still had keys to her apartment. Her thought was that he might put them to use now. Shagg was almost to Duke's car when Shorty spoke up.

"You wanna go with me to my apartment? I can fix you something to eat, and we can get some sleep."

Duke had a real good feeling that cooking and sleeping weren't all that was on Shorty's mind.

"Drop me off at Shorty's spot and tell sis where I'm at."

She gave Shagg directions, and he had no problem finding her apartment complex. Shorty got out to open the front door and make sure everything was safe before Duke got out. She held the door open for him.

"You got a nice li'l spot," he told her, looking around.

"It's OK."

Duke stopped dead in his tracks as he surveyed the pictures on the wall. He couldn't believe his eyes. It just couldn't be. Shorty was in the kitchen cooking and didn't notice him enter the kitchen.

"What the fuck is this?" he spat out, holding a Glock 17 in one hand and the picture he took off the wall in the other.

Shorty looked back over her shoulder. "It's a picture that I took at my job," she told him and went back to doing what she was doing as if it wasn't a big deal.

"You a fucking cop."

"No, I'm not. I am a narcotics agent . . . then why you tripping?"

Duke dropped the picture on the counter and turned to walk away, but she put her hand on his shoulder.

"I'm not trying to bust you . . . boy, you are way out of our league." Shorty started smiling, but she saw that Duke wasn't laughing. "I really don't know."

"OK, you work for Metro Narcotics. I want a list of the upcoming busts that they're planning to make. Don't try to tell me that you can't do it because I know that you can."

It was after 8:00 a.m. by the time Shorty finished cooking.

She fixed his plate, cleaned the kitchen, and went to take a shower. Duke had a fat blunt in his mouth and stacks of money laid out on the bed when she came out of the bathroom.

"I know dam well all of that money ain't come out of your pocket. You got to be crazy or asking to be robbed."

"It may be a li'l bit of both."

He unstrapped the vest and slid the twin Glock 17 pistols under the pillow. Duke wrapped rubber bands around the money and put it on the nightstand. Shorty stood in front of him wearing a red see-through teddy. Duke tried to act like he didn't see the look in her eyes, but it was obvious. Although he was a hustler and she was a police officer, Shorty could prove to be useful. If she was an undercover agent, he was finished; but if not, he now had an eye inside of Metro Narcotics.

"How I look?" Shorty asked, spinning in a model gesture.

He reached underneath her gown and grabbed a handful of her ass. "You know I'ma kill you if you working undercover, huh," he whispered in her ear.

"And what if I'm not?"

"It's only one way to find out."

Shorty pushed Duke back onto the bed and used her tongue to touch him from head to toe. She then climbed on top of him and rode him like a thoroughbred horse. He thought that she was finished, but Shorty only turned around and rode him reverse cowgirl. As soon as Duke got on top, he took the rubber off. Shorty felt the difference as soon as he push deep inside of her.

"What are you doing, put the rubber back on."

"I'm putting insurance on my claim, now turn your back ass over."

He worked every bone in Shorty's five-foot-three 130-pound body. He didn't take a break until over three hours later. Duke knew that he had put it down because Shorty was sound asleep when he came back into the room. He went to sleep and didn't wake up until six that evening. The first thing that he did was reach under the pillow. Not feeling the guns almost made him have a heart attack. Duke didn't look over at the nightstand because he knew that the money was gone. His instincts told him to chill because he could hear soft music and smell food. The bedroom door flew open, and he sat up. Shorty stood in the doorway holding a tray with food on it.

"You don't need to drink or smoke because you sleep like a dead man, and yo eyes be open." She saw the look on his face and knew why he was looking like that.

"Take this food that I took my time to cook, Duke. I don't appreciate you testing me because I'm not a little gurl."

"You could have took that shit, I ain't tripping. Fifty grand is nothing compared to the life that I can give you. Now can I have my guns back. I don't like feeling naked."

"Am I gonna see you again, because I'm on vacation, and I would love to spend more time with you."

"I'ma let you get that list for me, and then you gone see me."

Shorty went over to her walk-in closet and came out with his stuff.

"Oh yeah, your phones will drive somebody crazy. As soon as one stops ringing, another one starts ringing."

Someone named Shawn came over here too. I told her that I was not waking you up, and she said she would be back at 7:00 p.m."

Duke looked down at his watch and heard the honking of a car horn.

"That's my sister . . . I gotta go, but I'a be back in a few days or so."

"You really coming back?"

"I said—"

"I know what you said, but I also know that you . . . you have a flock of women. I'm not trying to be another one of your one-night- stands."

"Call me."

"Hold up." Shorty grabbed the plate off the tray and put foil paper over it. "When I cook for you, you gone eat it."

He gave her a kiss on the cheek and took the plate out her hand. Duke took the steps two steps at a time. Shawn was waiting in a brand-new Jaguar XJ8L.

"You late, and you taking forever," she told him when he opened the door.

"I was sleep," he said, adjusting his seat.

Shawn shook her head. "Why you over here in this neighborhood? You already know that these niggaz don't like you over here."

"You gone find me a spot over by the college, then. I need at least three bedrooms and a two-car garage."

"All you think about is a new piece of pussy. Boy, these hoes is gone be the death of you."

*   *   *   *   *

Chapter 15
Wins and Losses

Duke got out of bed and stretched his arms high above his head. He put on a pair of Gucci slippers and took the elevator downstairs to the kitchen. His mind was racing as he sat down at the circular marble counter. So much had happened in the past four years of his life. He was twenty times richer, but he also had enough problems to drive a man plum crazy. There was nothing that he couldn't have, yet everything seemed so stressful. He lit a blunt and went to his office.

He hadn't been in this room a hundred times, but it held a million secrets. Once this home was finally finished being built, Duke couldn't believe that it was the same house that he had dreamed up: 9011 hsf, lbr, 10½ bth, vintage and imported furniture, with state-of-the-art appliances and hundreds of thousands of dollars' worth of marble. The security system that he had installed would make Fort Knox jealous. A party boat and a 120-foot yacht sat docked at the pier behind the house. All seven acres were fenced off, and every one of the nine garage doors had something exclusive behind it.

A thick cloud of yellow smoke settled over his head as the office door eased open. His wife-to-be came into the room and floated across the pillow-soft carpet. He had his head down, so he didn't see her come in.

"Back to this 4:00 a.m. shit, huh."

Duke put a smile on his face before looking up. "I had some figures to look over. Plus, I got a lot on my mind right now."

"I knew you was down here when I rolled over to hold you and you were gone. What's wrong?"

Looking into her eyes, he knew why any man would be happy to have her until death tore them apart. She was perfect in her own way, and very independent. What more could a man ask for from a woman who was ready to ride or die for him? She took the blunt out of his hand and ran her manicured nails across his head.

"You need to stop by my shop and get this cut."

"La-La—"

"Shush."

He kissed the nape of her neck and rubbed the moist spot between her legs.

"Shawn said pick her up at 2:00 p.m. She said that ya'll got a plane to catch, and she don't want to be late.

La-La was nodding her head, but catching a plane was the last thing on her mind. She had a burning sensation inside of her body that only Duke could put out. He pulled the wifebeater over her head, picked La-La up, and sat her on the edge of the white marble desktop. She opened the robe he had on and pulled it until it was in a pile on the floor. They locked up like two animals on a kill-or-be-killed mission. Duke pushed deep inside of her, and La-La clawed at his back, meeting his every stroke.

*   *   *   *

Shagg didn't know what to do. He was six figures short on Duke's money and knew how that would play out. It wasn't that he didn't have the money; Shagg just didn't want to go in his stash. He'd have to resort to his last resources to get the money back that he'd lost in Vegas. Shagg drove over to Money's car lot, sitting on the corner of Apple Street and South Second Street. The car lot was filled with all types of vehicles, most of which were already tricked out. All you had to do was crank up and go.

"I see you got the Bentley looking like new money," he replied, referring to Shagg's Chrysler 300C.

"It's all right."

"Let's have a drink."

Shagg declined the drink and followed Money into the back to his office. This was by far not your average car dealership—everything about it said dope boy. The only people who bought cars from Money were drug dealers; a white person wouldn't dare be caught on a lot like this one. They walked into Money's office, and Shagg's eyes went straight to the camera mounted in the corner.

"What the camera for?"

"Tha shit don't work, boy. I put that up there to scare people."

Shagg didn't know what to think, but right now, it really didn't matter."

"I need them thangs."

"You still want 10 kilos?" he asked, looking at Shagg.

"Yep."

Money pointed to a box sitting in the far corner of the room. "It's over there, you can give me the money in a couple days."

This nigga cooler than I thought, Shagg thought to himself.

"Look, I cut for you, homie, and I wanna see you do good. I'ma make you a offer that you can't refuse. I got a three-bedroom crib on Pargue that I really need to sell. If you buy the house I'a give you that blue C-class Benz outside. All you gotta do is give me seventy grand and I'a sign it over to you."

Shagg couldn't believe his ears. This was too good to be true. He already had plenty of real estate, but this was a three-bedroom house and a free Benz. He pulled two stacks of money out and dropped them on the desk.

"Here go fifty grand, I'ma give you the rest when I pay you for them bricks."

"You ain't gotta be in no rush. Just sign this, and I'ma fix up the paperwork," he said, pushing sheets of paper across the desk.

Money grabbed the keys from behind the desk on the wall and tossed them to Shagg.

"These the house keys, but the Benz want be ready until tomorrow."

"Dam, Money, how a nigga tell you no. If you keep this up, me and you gone be working together full-time."

He stood up and extended his hand out to Shagg. "I hope so."

Shagg grabbed the box and closed the door when he left out. Money picked up the phone and turned the speaker phone off.

"Did you get that?"

"Good job, Money," the voice said.

"When do I get my bread, then?"

"Meet me downtown on Washington Street at midnight."

*   *   *   *   *

A wave of fear shot through his body like an electric volt as he drove through Plantation Apartments. Duke pressed the button under the dashboard, and an MP5 popped out. He refused to be caught slipping. He put Snooppy's number on speed dial to see if she was having company. A familiar candy-red Suburban couldn't be parked in front of her apartment building by coincidence. Duke wasn't mad that she was messing around, but she wasn't doing it where he paid bills. Where he hid his dope and sometimes lay his head. The phone rang ten times before she finally answered.

"Hello."

"Bitch . . . fuck is you doing?"

"Who is this?"

He was about to get out of the car but had to see what was going on first.

"I don't know what type of games you playing, but I ain't in the mood."

Snooppy waved to get Tocky and Nard's attention." Hey baby, how was your trip?"

This hoe must think that I'm dumb or something, he thought to himself. "What took you so long to answer the phone? You got company or some shit?

"I was in the shower . . . why, you coming over to see me today?"

I'ma kill this bitch, he told himself. "I'm on my way over there right now, bye."

Snooppy jumped right up and started to clean up the living room. It would take him at least an hour to get on that side of town; she knew that he had plenty of time.

"Ya'll gotta go because that nigga is on his way over here. I'ma call you a li'l later."

Tocky grabbed a handful of her ass and stared into her eyes. "Page me and put that code in when that nigga go to sleep."

She pressed her lips against his as he opened the front door. "Next time you come, don't bring yo homeboy. You know I like to fuck in private."

"Yea right, you freaky bitch," Tocky said, walking off.

Duke wanted to open fire, but the neighbors' children were running back and forth. It would bring too much heat if a kid got shot. Once the Suburban was out of sight, he got out of the car. Duke slid his key in the lock and slowly pushed the door open. The smell of pussy, weed, and alcohol hit him like a ton of bricks. He knew then that she was in the bathroom washing the smell of dick off of her body and breath. He opened the closet door and snatched every piece of clothing that belonged to Snooppy off of its hanger.

Snooppy was in the bathroom singing her heart out and didn't have the slightest idea that Duke was even in the apartment. As soon as he sat down on the bed, his cell phone started ringing.

"Hello."

"Can I see you?" a sweet voice asked.

"I'm glad that you call me. I need you to vacate the lease on that apartment that you rented in Plantation Apartments."

"Baby, what's wrong, did—"

"Just do what I said, and I a see you tonight," he told her and hung up.

Snooppy came out of the bathroom and almost had a heart attack when she saw Duke sitting on the bed. She saw her clothes scattered all over the place and knew that she was in trouble.

"Why—"

He jumped up from the bed and slapped Snooppy so hard that she flew back into the bathroom. Grabbing a handful of her hair, Duke snatched Snooppy back up onto her feet. Her body was shining like a diamond in the rough, but he could care less about that. He put the gun to her head and cocked the hammer back.

"Please . . . I'm sorry, I ain't—"

He slapped her. "You knew what was up, and you went along with it because you a jealous-hearted bitch."

He let go of her hair and walked out of the room. By the time he made it into the kitchen, Snooppy wrapped both of her arms around him in a deadlock.

"Please, don't do me like this, please . . . please . . ."

He kissed Snooppy on the neck and ran a hand down her voluptuous body, finding the moist spot between her legs. As her body began to relax, she loosened her death grip. He pushed

Snooppy off of him and, in one swift motion, snatched the fire extinguisher off of the wall and sprayed the whole bottle on her.

"Get out befo I kill you, you funky pussy bitch."

Snooppy made an attempt to crawl toward the door, looking like a roach on its deathbed. He saw that Snooppy was taking her time and kicked her in the crack of her ass. The neighbors' children stood around wide-eyed, looking at a naked Snooppy crawling on the pavement.

"Now go tell that nigga Tocky I said get at me."

*　　*　　*　　*　　*　　*

The nozzle on his operation was stripped, and the money was pouring in. Duke was making so much money that he had to buy houses just to store it in. Dre sent him 500 kilos to hold him over until the next re-up. As bad as he wanted to stop hustling, he couldn't. The type of money he was making was too addictive to walk away from. After you make so much money, it's more about the power and no longer about the money.

Duke backed the Escalade EXT up inside of Will's garage and took the duffel bags out. Will said that Trina was gone, so he could use his house to cut and recompress the kilos. He heard music when he unlocked the back door.

"Somebody in here?"

Duke didn't get a response, so he shut the blinds and started breaking down bricks. Twenty minutes later, he was still recompressing bricks. Duke wasn't paying any attention at first, but then he realized that someone was controlling the music. He walked to the back of the house where the music was coming from and found Will's bedroom door wide open.

"Ahh . . . ahh . . . ahhh," Trina screamed, scrambling for something to cover up with.

"My bad," Duke told her, turning to walk away. The sight of Trina's naked body made him want to fuck her, his best friend's girlfriend. Now he was regretting that he had asked Will to use his house. Duke was in the kitchen duct-taping up kilos when Trina walked in.

"Oh hell, nah, what the hell is you doing?"

"What it look like?"

"How you get in here?"

"Will gave me his keys so that I can get in, because he said that you would be gone. I'm sorry for walking in on you like that, but you ain't supposed to be sitting around naked."

"You must of forgot that this is my house." She came over to where he stood and let the robe she had on fall to the floor. "I can do what the fuck I want."

Duke knew that fucking Trina was wrong, but he felt like Will would do it to him if he got the chance. He picked Trina up and took her in the bedroom. Duke laid her facedown on the bed to hide the guilt, because he couldn't look in her eyes as they exchanged fuck faces.

"Ooh, Duke . . . yes . . . yes . . . ooh . . . Duke," she screamed, looking over her shoulder.

Trina never told Duke that Lanny was in the room across the hall asleep. Lanny jumped up when she heard the scream and bed clapping. She couldn't tell whether she was dreaming or not, but she was most definitely about to find out. Lanny put her ear to Trina's door, and all she could hear was moaning. She eased the door open, and her mouth hit the floor. Duke had Trina facedown with her ass in the air.

"Ya'll is so dam wrong."

Duke continued to long-stroke Trina as Lanny kept running her mouth. Trina tried to tell him to stop when she heard Lanny's voice, but he was slamming deep inside of her. Duke felt the nut coming and pulled out, shooting cum all over Trina's ass and back. He then put on his clothes and left the room without even saying bye. He ran into Lanny in the kitchen.

"What's up?" he asked, giving her a big smile.

"You some shit! I hope yo fucking dick fall off, because you always sticking it in somebody's woman. Oh, I forgot, that's what friends are for."

"You lucky that I don't want you." He pointed a finger in her face. "I'a have yo pretty ass fucking, sucking, cooking, cleaning, and staying in the house."

"I would never fuck you, nigga. Yo money and street fame don't mean shit to me."

Duke pulled a stack of purple one-hundred-dollar bills out of his pocket "Bitch, I can buy you." He threw the money in her face. "Take that and go treat yoself because I'ma have you eating dick befo long."

*   *   *   *

"Where you at?"

"I'm at one of my spots. Look, I need you to go to Parkview to go check on Diron. I just got a call, and they say he out there fighting."

"I'a check on it, I'm already headed out that way. When you gone, brang me my change."

"It's gone be Monday or Tuesday."

"OK . . . oh yea, you need to go see yo moma."

Conrad set the stack of money down that he had been counting. "You my god-brother, not my daddy. I gotta go."

Diron was gone, and the fight was over by the time. Duke made it to Parkview. Hotboy told him that he was on his way, and Duke decided to walk around until he got there. It wasn't an everyday thing for Duke to be walking around the hood. Baze and Lowdown were trying their best to get put down.

"You need to gone put us down and let us show you that we can get to the money."

"What can you handle?" he asked, passing Baze the blunt.

"I don't know who these niggaz thank they is, but they ain't running shit around here. What's gone end up happening is somebody gona get killed."

Duke, Baze, and Lowdown looked back and forth at one another. Duke didn't think those words were meant for him, but they surely caught his attention. He looked back at Big P standing in the breezeway with some of his boys.

"You talking to me?" Duke asked, looking at Big P.

"Yea, you li'l bitch and I should slap the fuck out of you."

Duke took a few steps back because Big P was 300 pounds and stood over six feet tall.

"You got me fucked up."

Big P cocked back to hit Duke with the beer bottle that he had been drinking out of, and he saw the gun in Duke's hand.

"Oh, you got a gun. I'ma take that shit and make you eat it when I finish. Then I'ma go in yo pocket after I knock yo pussy ass out."

The gun went off, and Big P fell faster than the Twin Towers. Everyone standing around stood frozen in total shock.

"You better kill me," he spat out, looking up at Duke. "You a dead man walking if you let me alive."

Duke put the gun to his head. "Say one mo fucking word, and I'ma knock yo brain all over this sidewalk. Say something . . . say something, nigga."

He turned to walk away, and people started running in his direction. Duke swung around, pointing the gun in their direction.

"Get back . . . get back . . . get the fuck back."

His blood was boiling, and his adrenaline was pumping as he ran over to Daja's apartment. Grabbing the AK-47 out of the closet, his intention was to kill everyone standing in front of Building 17. Daja met him on the stairs and grabbed hold of the barrel of the gun.

"What the fuck is wrong with you? You about to throw it all away for these nothing-as niggas. You need to leave because the police is on they dam way out here."

He let her take the gun out of his hand and ran downstairs. Duke took the Benz to storage and took out one of his trucks. The pistol that he shot Big P with found its way to the trashcan after being wiped off.

"Hello."

"You all right?"

"I'm good, Aunt Roz."

The line went silent for a moment. "The police and news reporters are outside. I don't think you should come over here."

"I'm not. I—"

"They say you are armed and dangerous, baby. They plan on shooting you if you don't turn yo self in."

Duke stubbed out the blunt, reached out and lit another blunt." What yo think I should do, because I'm thinking about flying to Mi—"

"Just sit tight and get your thoughts together. Shawn gone come pick you up in a li'l while."

"You know I love you, huh?"

"I love you too."

As soon as he hung up, LaLa passed him one of his other phones.

"Hello."

"What the fuck happen?"

"The nigga start tripping, and I shot him."

"So what's yo next move because you on the news?" Duke saw La-La on the phone and knew that she was talking to Shawn or Ms. Washington.

"I'ma turn myself in, and then we gone have a meeting once I come home."

"You want me to bond you out?"

"Nah, you just have my bread when I come home."

Duke turned himself in and didn't get a bond until two days later. The judge gave him a half of a million-dollar bail. Everyone in his dorm thought that he was a sitting duck. To their surprise, his bail was posted forty-five minutes later.

Chapter 16
All Money Ain't Good

A nice-looking female was situated behind the front desk when Shagg walked through the door. He turned the charm on as he made his way over to her.

"Have I walked into heaven or—"

"Money in the back waiting on you," she said with a smile.

He wanted to ask her about lunch but decided to take care of business first. There would be plenty of time to get at her. Shagg walked down the long hallway and tapped on a door with the letters HNIC written on it in bold letters.

"Come in."

Shagg pushed the door open, and the stacks of money sitting on the desk immediately caught his attention. Something else caught his attention too, the man sitting next to Money's desk.

"My nigga, how life been treating you?" Money asked, walking around the desk.

"It's good." He pointed at the money on the desk. "Is that me?"

"Fasho . . . I want you to meet my man, Rylon."

"What up?"

Shagg set the bag on the desk and slid it over to Money. Money unzipped the bag to show Rylon what was in it.

"I ain't seen yo boy Duke in a minute. What, he hiding out or something?"

Shagg went numb at the mention of Duke's name. He wanted to grab the bag and just leave. Duke's words were ringing inside of his head.

If you fucking with that police ass, nigga, I'ma kill you.

"I ain't tryna rush you, but I got somewhere to be."

Rylon gave Money a sideways glance because he didn't want this deal to be blown. Once he took down Duke's operation, he was guaranteed to get a promotion. So there was no way that he was going to let a lowlife like Money ruin that. Rylon grabbed one of the Ziploc bags out of the bag off of the desk.

"Is it all there?"

"Ten hard and ten soft," Shagg said, looking at him.

"Is the dope any good, because there is some big-ass cookies."

"That right there," Shagg said, pointing at the Ziploc bag in his hand. "That's the best dope in the state of Louisiana, and I can put my life on that."

"Well, look, can I come straight to you the next time? Money said that he gone be out of town, and I'ma need to re-up in three days. If it's cool, you could give me your number, and I'a call you when I get in town."

Shagg raked the money into a Walmart bag and wrote his number down. "Hit me up." He passed the paper to Rylon on his way out of the door.

Rylon pressed Eject on the hidden camera behind Money's desk and put the CD inside the bag with the dope.

"If you blow my case, I'ma kill you. If he wants to tell you about Duke, let him, but don't ever press him for information."

Rylon walked out and left Money standing there looking stupid.

*   *   *   *

Heads were turning as Shagg pulled into the parking lot of Club Shakers. He parked the Challenger SRT8 and went in the club. He found Will setting up tables in the VIP area.

"What's the deal?" he asked, giving Will a brotherly hug.

"Why he rent the club on a Saturday night, he—"

142

"Ain't no use in use talking about it because you know how Conrad is."

"Well, where yo liquor at?"

Shagg slapped the top of his forehead. "You know what, that shit is still in my trunk. Come on, come help me get this shit."

A powder-blue 750Li pulled up to the front door of the club just as they were coming out.

"Yea, I know I look good," Diron said, hopping out.

"You straight," Will said, smiling.

"Help me get this shit out of the car. Conrad ass still ain't made it yet."

"You know dam well that he the first one to set something up and the last—" Shagg tapped the screen on his phone and started to laugh. "This that nigga right here . . . Hello."

"Where y'all at?"

"We at the club, where you at?"

"Coming down the street," he said and hung up.

Every baller in Monroe came to or stopped by Club Shakers on Saturday nights. If you were somebody or wanted to be somebody, Shakers was the place for you. Word spread that Conrad was throwing a baller bash, and it brought out the whole city. Not a word was said about the two-hundred-dollar cover charge, because everything else was free. A platinum-gray Suburban blocked one end of the street off, and everyone braced themselves to see what would happen next. A 1996 maroon Chevy Impala peeled rubber, and time stopped when Conrad emerged from the cloud of smoke. The medium burl wood Revolution 4.1 Dalvin rims were about to spin off of the car when he put his foot on the brake. Conrad put the chinchilla hood over his head and opened the door. Shagg cut through the gathering crowd and put an arm around Conrad's neck.

"Nigga, this is too darn much. You can't be doing that shit that Duke be going. This is a signature on all of our federal indictment."

"I'm feeling like a boss right now, I gotta act like one.

Conrad hadn't been in the club five minutes, and he was already ready to leave. Gold diggers wouldn't quite be coming to his table, and niggas kept asking for handouts.

"This is a nice party."

"It's all right," he said, turning toward the voice.

"Me and my home gurls wanna know where the after-party gone be at. You know, the one where the grown folks gone be at."

He gave her a sideways look." Who are you? You just standing in front of my table and ain't told me yo name or nothing."

"I'm Lizzy." She turned to the two women standing behind her. "This is Jeri, and that's Sarah."

Lizzy and Jeri were average, but Sarah was fine enough to turn a gay man straight. She saw Conrad looking at her and took a step closer so he could get a better look.

"Meet me at the Baymont off of I-20 when they close."

"You gone bring—"

"I'ma holla."

Before the three women were out of his sight, a dime piece sat down next to him.

"Dam, you got all of your hoes in the house tonight. It's like a pimp, huh."

"It's cold, but I'm guessing that it's fair. I don't see you shaking yo ass, so what brought you out tonight?"

"I'm pregnant."

Conrad spat Patron and cranberry juice all over the table.

"And yo brother want you to have a abortion, huh."

"He said that you took advantage of me . . . but—"

"Fuck Tocky, what do you want?"

"I want me and you to be a couple, but I know you ain't gone give me that."

Conrad was sobering up with every word that came out of Gwen's mouth.

"You ain't killing my baby, and that's the end of that. Better yet, tell yo brother to holla at me."

I knew I should of just got an abortion like Tocky said. Now I'm in the middle of an ongoing drug war, she thought, looking at Conrad. He read the look on her face and knew what she was thinking.

"I'a move you to a new spot and give you whatever, but you ain't killing my seed."

"Conrad."

"I don't give a dam if God told you to. I said no, and that's what I mean."

She put her hand on top of his. "Don't make me choose between you and my brotha. I told you that we shouldn't have had sex, but you don't know what 'no' means. Now look at what we gotta deal with."

I know she ain't blaming me. This bitch chase me down for the dick. I ain't gone bring that up, though. I'ma put my foot in her once she have that baby, Conrad thought to himself.

"Look, we in the wrong place to be holding this type of conversation. Let me finish—"

"I can't deal with these hoes being disrespectful. Like the hoe in the pink right there." She pointed to a female on the dance floor. "Bitch been hawking me since I sat down."

He let his eyes roam the room, stopping on Pretty. Conrad knew that she wasn't crazy enough to clown him in public, but Gwen didn't know that. The tears started to fall as she stood up to leave.

"I'ma kill yo brother if you kill my baby." He grabbed her by the arm. "I'ma good nigga, and you know it, but don't play with my feelings. Now, take yo sexy ass home and call me in the morning.

Gwen put her hand over her face. It was either kill the baby to please Tocky or keep the baby to please Conrad. She was running low on choices, and things only seemed to be getting worse.

"Oh you major now, huh. I know you the only one in here with the nuts to buy a Bentley," she said, sitting back down.

"That's a company car," he told her with a smile.

Gwen saw Netta coming through the crowd and was happy that she'd stayed. She unstrapped the five-inch heels and stood up.

"I don't want you fighting with my baby in you. Let me handle my own hoes."

She threw her earrings down on the table. "Don't trip, I'ma make yo hoes respect me and mine."

Gwen hit Netta in the mouth with a right hook as soon as she made it within arm's reach, they were punching, kicking, scratching, biting and pulling at one another's hair. The fight took a drastic turn when Netta fell on the floor. Gwen was stomping a mud hole in her until someone punched her from behind. The left hook took her by surprise, and she lost her balance.

"You wanna break it up?" Shagg asked, passing Conrad a blunt.

Before he could answer, all hell broke loose. Netta tried to punch Gwen and almost lost her arm.

Netta staggered back. "That bitch cut me."

Gwen stood up waving a broken Cristal bottle like a knife, opening up everything that she touched. Netta tried to run, but

Gwen ran her down and cut gashes in her back. Security rushed through the crowd and snatched the broken bottle from Gwen.

"Let me go." She elbowed the security guard. "You wasn't trying to hold them hoes when they was jumping me."

The guard was squeezing Gwen against his chest, but she was still fighting him. Conrad stood up and hit him across the head with a Moet bottle. The lights came on, and everyone start running.

Conrad was holding a gun. "Gone leave, G. I don't want you to get shot."

Gwen ran out of the exit without another word. Conrad looked through the crowd and saw everyone but Diron.

A girl who looked far too young to be inside of a club walked up to him. "You Conrad?"

"Why, who wanna know?"

Her eyes dropped to the crispy white Reeboks on her feet.

"My cousin told me to tell you that yo brother is outside fighting."

He gave her a hundred-dollar bill. "Thank you."

Will and Shagg stood up when they saw Conrad coming their way, gun in hand.

"What up?"

"Come on," he told them and turned to walk away.

You couldn't tell who was who because over four thousand people were standing around. Conrad finally spotted Diron, Shagg, and Will and plowed through the crowd. He was leaning up against a car breathing hard.

"Who you fighting?"

Diron took a moment to catch his breath. "Nard and Tocky tried to jump me."

"Here," he said, giving him a gun.

Boom . . . Boom . . . Boom . . . Boom . . . Boom . . .
Boom . . . Boom . . .

The crowd parted like the Red Sea when the cannon came to life. Diron ran behind Nard but still didn't hit him. He let loose the whole clip and stopped running. Conrad ran past him and let off ten shots. Nard's body hit the ground. Conrad put a new clip in the gun, and someone grab hold of his arm. He swung around and put the gun in that person's face.

"The . . . the police is coming," Sarah said, shaking.

"Stick this in yo purse," he demanded, giving her the gun.

Shagg was in the middle of the parking lot shooting an MP5 when Conrad and Sarah ran around the building.

"Let's go . . . let's go . . . let's go, nigga."

Conrad hit the remote start on the Bentley, and they jumped in. "Meet me at the Baymont."

*   *   *   *   *   *

Chapter 17
The Good Die Young

Boxes of money were stacked up from wall to wall. Duke felt like he was part of the United States Treasury Department. Since he had been home, all he had been doing was counting money. He had a meeting set up to break the news to the crew. Once these last keys ran out, he was giving the game up. La-La came through his office door holding a blunt, dressed in a pink-and-white fishnet bodysuit.

"Will came by my shop and told me that you were fucking Trina."

Duke stopped sorting through the piles of dollar bills. "Did he try to fuck?"

"Yep, he said he had some money for you. Wanted me to give him the address to our house too."

"Put some fucking clothes on and lock this room up. I'a be back."

Everyone but Will was waiting at Shawn's house when he showed up. Duke was so mad that he almost ran into the back of Conrad's brand-new BMW. He knew that he was wrong for having sex with Trina, and nothing would justify that. Although he had given Will 10 kilos to get on his feet and then gave him 50 kilos a month from that point on. So he felt obligated to have anything that Will had. Shawn knew something was wrong when she came outside.

"All I wanna know is why he trying to go to my house while I'm in jail?" he said, looking around at everyone.

"Don't be clowning at my house."

"Ain't nobody finna do no clowning. We having a nice and calm family meeting."

Shawn saw the look in his eyes and knew Duke was up to something but just didn't know exactly what.

"Don't try to play me crazy. You say all ya'll about to do is talk, that's all ya'll better do."

"Take all of the women in the house with you," he told her when he saw Will's midnight-blue Jag turn the corner.

"Trina, the women are in the house," Duke told her when they got out of the car.

Duke walk over to where Will was and took a seat next to him at the patio table.

"Why you asking my gurl for my address and I ain't even give you my address? Then you told her that me and Trina is fucking."

Will looked from Duke to Trina. The look in Duke's eyes told him that they were guilty.

"Tell him, Will. Tell Duke what you said you was planning on doing. You wanna beat on me, but you want stand up to him. Look at you, you no—"

Will slapped Trina in the mouth, and she fell out of the chair into the ground.

"I'm not talking to you, so shut the fuck up. Duke fuc—"

Will didn't see the pistol until it came crashing down on top of his head. He tried to run, but Duke was all over him. Shawn ran out of the house and wrestled the pistol away from him.

"Duke, you need to leave because I told you not to clown in my dam yard."

"You gone pistol-whip me because you fuck my bitch. I swear to God that you gone get yo issue."

Duke tried to take the pistol from Shawn, but she threw it up on top of the house.

"You ain't finna make this house hot like you did the last one. I don't give a dam cuzz you paid for it, either, you and all of yo company need to leave."

Duke wanted to argue but bit down on his bottom lip.

"Say, let's get out of her yard."

* * * *

La-La and Duke were coming out of the Pecanland Mall when Daja passed by.

"Hey, Duke," she said, smiling from ear to ear.

He waved and kept walking, but she followed him out of the mall.

"Oh, you too good to speak now."

"Baby, do you know her?" LaLa asked looking back.

"She ain't nobody worth talking about. Go get in the car."

Daja continued to follow them, pointing, talking loud, and causing a scene. Duke tried to ignore her, but she just wouldn't go away.

"Take yo stupid ass back in the mall before you piss me off."

La-La took her heels off just as Daja ran up. Duke stepped between them and put his hand in her face.

"La-La, I told you to get in the car. Now get in the fucking car like I told you." He turned back to Daja and put a hand on her shoulder. "Let me tell you some, bitch. They gone find yo nasty ass somewhere stanking, if you ever clown me in public again."

"But, Duke—"

"Bitch, when you see me wit the wifey, you don't say shit to me."

With that being said, he got in the car and drove off. Conrad and Diron were the closest thing that he had to family in the streets. He had a lot of respect for Hotboy and Shagg, but it

151

was more out of love than trust. Duke knew that he could trust his god-brothers, though. That's why he didn't regret doing anything for them. Everyone was standing in front of Cent's house when Duke turned down Allen Street. Hotboy, Shagg, and Conrad were leaning against brand-new 760Li Beemers. Diron was sitting in a new black-on-black Dodge Viper, rolling blunts. The Artic White Phantom came to a stop in front of them, and all they could see was the hands on the steering wheel.

"Does anyone have any hydro?"

They burst out laughing. "Fasho," everyone said in unison.

"Let's pass through the carwash before we smash the club. Every thang on me tonight."

He drove off, and the cars began to file in behind him. Little did they know, cameras were flashing down the street. The carwash was jam-packed when they drove up. This is what they considered the pre-club show. If you were ridin' clean and wanted to be seen, this was the place to be.

"Duke . . . das you?"

"What do you think?" he asked, turning to face the voice.

"I don't know, I heard you was on yo dick."

In Monroe, people gossiped about any and everything. If they don't know, they will assume until they think they have it all figured out.

"Do it look like I'm doing bad."

"That mean them keys going for ten then, huh."

"Let's go," Duke said, looking at the crew. Necks were snapping trying to get a second look at the black and white foreign cars as they drove off. Duke was shining and knew that he deserved every moment of it. After losing soldiers and ducking feds every day, he was supposed to be the man. Nothing came to him for free, so he planned to live life to the fullest.

Men and women alike were staring when they came through the club entrance.

Duke had on so much ice that he was borderline frost bit. Golf balls in his ears, a glacier on his pinky, a necklace made of diamonds the size of dimes, and a medallion on it the size of a saucer. He was what jack boys consider a walking lick, but he wasn't worried about being robbed. He and his crew had Mark 23 handguns, and most of all, he had on a bulletproof vest. He had vowed to wear it even if it was hot outside. Although he was young, Duke had grown man money. People who have been in the game all their life wasn't getting it like him. Five hundred dollars got them in without being touched. Duke bought the bar and went to his reserved VIP section.

"Say, bartender, get these ladies whatever they drinking," he said, looking at the vultures starting to crowd around his table.

He looked through the sea of faces and saw a face that he hadn't seen in years. Duke couldn't remember her name, but he remembered that body.

"What's your name?" he asked, tapping her on the shoulder.

"I'm Daysha . . . why, who are you?"

"Oh, you don't know who I am, but you staring all in my face."

"I can't remember your name, but I believe me and you use to talk."

Conrad and Diron were in the dice room. All bets automatically went up to two hundred dollars when they walked in the room. Diron hit 8 naturals and 6 of his 7 points. He was so hot on the dice that the houseman started cheating. Conrad took over where he left off at and broke the dice game up.

"Let me hold something," they said, crowding around.

"Hell no, remember when the shoe was on the other foot? Well, kick rocks," Diron said, pulling Conrad toward the door.

Duke was still sitting in the same spot that he had been sitting in for the past hour.

"You telling me that you remember me but you don't know my name."

"Yep, that's about right."

"Where you been the last five years?"

"I moved to Dallas four years ago because Monroe is just too small for me."

"How long you plan to be in town?"

Daysha's eyes were glued to the sparkling diamonds on his neck. "I'ma be here until next week. Why, you got a reason why I should stay longer?"

"Didn't you say that you gone do hair?"

"Nah, I said I'm the best hairdresser that you gone find."

Daysha had aged like wine over the past few years. She had really become a dime piece.

"How about you open a shop of your own?"

She looked at him crazy. "Where I'ma get that type of money from?"

"Don't worry about none of that shit, Shawty. Do you think you can run yo own business?"

"Even if I couldn't, do you think I would say no?"

"Hold up . . . Hello," he said, tapping the earpiece.

"Baby, the feds is on yo ass. They probaly following you right now. I made copies of the papers that they sent down to the station."

"We gone talk about this later because I'm at the club right now. I'ma call you as soon as I get home." He hung the phone up on her and turned back to Daysha.

"You gone spend the night with me?" she asked, licking her lips.

"How you gone ask me to spend the night with you and you don't even remember my name?"

"Duke . . . I should kick yo ass for hurt my feelings all them years ago. Now act like a regular nigga and come fuck me."

"I'm not these nigga." He waved his hand. "I'm still dat nigga, Daysha."

"Here." She passed him the key to her room. "Don't have me waiting for nothing. I wanna see if that stoke done improved."

He grabbed a handful of her Charmine-soft ass when she stood up to leave. Duke was planning on putting good use to the key in his hand. Outside, the club was just as packed as the inside. Duke reached out to open his car door and saw a familiar face. He pulled the gun out of his pants as he cut through the maze of cars. Duke hit him across the head with the pistol, and he hit the ground.

Shagg and Hotboy were waving pistols at the crowd. "Get back . . . everybody, get the fuck back."

Duke, Conrad, and Diron were stomping a mud hole in him. The woman with him started screaming.

"Ya'll gone kill him . . . Duke, please stop. I promise you that Will is gonna pay you yo money. I promise you."

The beating didn't stop until the owner of the club came outside and begged Duke to stop. They all left in separate directions and met back at Cent's house.

"I want everybody to switch cars and lay low for the rest of tonight. We gone all meet up tomorrow.

"Duke, let me drive yo car, and you can put mine in yo storage. I bring it to you tomorrow," Diron told him, smiling.

Diron was only sixteen, but he was living the life of a grown man. Aunt Roz had told Duke to keep him in school and out of trouble, but he had done the complete opposite. Duke let him do whatever he wanted to do and gave him everything that he asked for. Conrad and Diron both owned houses, stores. They trailed one another to the highway and began to go their separate ways. As they were going their separate ways, a black Cadillac pulled alongside the Phantom and opened fire with machine guns. The driver of the Phantom slumped over the steering wheel, and the car rolled out into the middle of the intersection. An 18-wheeler blindsided the Phantom, knocking it into the ditch.

Duke had always felt that his crew was untouchable, until that very moment, his life started to flash before his eyes when the gunshots sounded off, but he wasn't dead. Hotboy and Duke made a U-turn in the middle of the highway. Shagg and Conrad were long gone before the first shot was even fired. Duke got out of the car and ran down in the ditch. Hotboy was right on his heels screaming at someone on his cell phone. An ambulance just so happened to be passing by and stopped to see what was going on.

"What's the problem?"

"Bitch, don't you see that my baby brother is trapped in this fucking car!" he screamed, pulling on the smashed door.

"Calm down, sir."

Duke wanted to strangle him. "Bitch, don't tell me to calm down. You better call somebody to help me get my brother cut out of this car, or I'ma hurt you."

Hotboy stood as far away from Duke as he could. He was still hurting, but he didn't want to get in Duke's way. By the time they finally got Diron out of the car, Duke was hysterical. Tears were running down his cheeks like he had a faucet inside of his eye socket.

"Cover him up . . . I said cover him up!" Duke said, grabbing one of the paramedics by the neck.

Diron was pronounced dead on arrival. Duke couldn't think of the right words to tell Aunt Roz that her son was dead. Everyone in the waiting room sat staring at him like he was going crazy. He paced the floor, kicking over trash cans and punching holes in walls.

"Why . . . why?" he kept asking himself, beating on his chest.

He was so caught up that he didn't see Aunt Roz, Shagg, Shawn, and Conrad when they came in.

"What's going on?" Aunt Roz asked, looking around.

No one said a word; they were waiting for Duke to do all of the explaining. Aunt Roz saw how bloody Duke was and knew that something bad had happened.

"They shot him . . . they . . . they shot him."

"Who, who shot who?" she asked, looking confused.

"He dead . . . Diron, they shot him." His tear well dried up when he saw the look on her face. "I didn't mean for it to happen. It just happen so fast that—"

She slapped him. "What the fuck did you do? Why you doing this to me?" She slapped him again. "What the fuck did you do to my baby?"

Duke tried to hug her, but she pushed him away and continued to slap him across the face.

"Muthafucka, get off of me," she screamed, pushing him away. "Why Duke . . . why . . . why you had my baby out there selling that shit? He was sixteen, Duke, sixteen—"

"I ain't mean to, I promise—"

"Don't give me that shit, nigga. What type of heartless shit is that?"

He tried to reach for her, but she pushed his arms away. "I . . . I . . . I—"

"Get yo no-good ass out of my face befo I kill you."

Conrad, Duke, Hotboy, and Shagg went out in the hallway. They conversed about who, what, when, where, and how it was about to go down. Conrad didn't say a word; he was crying on Duke's shoulder.

"I want all these niggaz dead. Kill everybody that got beef wit us, niggas and hoes." He pushed Conrad off him and walked over to the elevator. "I can't believe that I'm 'bout to bury Diron."

* * * * *

After a week of smoking and drinking, that dreadful day had finally arrived. Family members from all over the United States came home to Monroe and paid their respects. Duke still couldn't understand the whole situation. His mind couldn't comprehend that he was actually burying Diron. A police had to clear a path so they could get the limos into the Monroe Civic Center parking lot. Duke and La-La got out of the first limo, and he realized then that it was true. This wasn't a dream: Diron was gone and wasn't coming back. Shawn got out of the second limo and held her hand out to help Aunt Roz as they were walking into the civic center. Aunt Roz passed out and collapsed to the ground. Duke and Conrad rushed over to help Shawn pick her up.

"Moma . . . get up!" Shawn said, tapping her cheek.

"Pick her up, we gotta get her to a hospital."

Shawn rode with Aunt Roz to the hospital and made them go inside of the funeral. Everyone took their seats, and the reverend made his way to the podium.

"How is everyone today?"

"All right," the room said in unison.

"As you all know, today we are here to lay a very young man to rest. God has called him to come home. Although this is a sad occasion, we should rejoice in the fact that he has moved on to a better place." The preacher took his glasses off. "I'm not here to pass judgment on any of you that I see in attendance, but bullets have no names on them. All I'm asking is, when will it stop? The drugs, murders, and all of the violence in the black communities across America. Nowadays we are not burying a man who has had the joy of enjoying life, we are burying children. Our doctors, lawyers, and future presidents." He took a sip from the glass of water before continuing, "We are selling ourselves short for expensive clothing, jewelry, and fancy cars, selling our souls." He gave his words time to sink in. "I'm not here to preach to you young men and women in attendance. I'm just asking you to open your eyes before it is too late. I want everyone to take a good look at this young man and think hard." He pointed to the casket. "If there is no change in our communities, that might end up being you."

All eyes were on Duke when he stood up to make his way down the aisle. He dropped down to his knees in front of the casket and cried like a baby. Hotboy, Shagg, La-La, and Conrad rushed over to try to help him up. To everyone's surprise, he didn't want to get up.

"I'm sorry, li'l brother . . . I'm sorry. I ain't mean for it to happen. Why they take you from—"

Gunshots erupted, and Duke dove across the floor, crawling under the casket. He could hear screaming and more gunshots, but he couldn't see what was going on. Five minutes later, the room was silent.

"You all right, son?" someone asked, putting a hand on his shoulder.

He turned over to see the preacher standing over him. Duke wiped the tears from his eyes and stood up.

"I need you to make sure that my brother gets to his gravesite. I'ma—"

"More killing want—"

"Man, I ain't tryna hear that shit," Duke told him before walking away.

No one got shot, but Diron's casket was riddled with bullet holes. Duke made La-La go home and met up with everyone else a block away from the civic center.

"I want her snatch from school and call me. Let's raise the body count before the sun rises."

*　　*　　*　　*

Duke and Hotboy drove through Oak Manor Apartments later that evening with ski masks on. They ran up to Tocky's sister's apartment and kicked the door in. They killed everyone including the dog before leaving. Nosy neighbors heard the gunshots and gathered around to see what was going on. Hotboy saw a crowd of people standing around, and he opened fire on them as they made their way back to the car.

"What?" Duke said, answering his phone.

"We got her."

"Hold on." He dialed Will's cell number. "I got yo li'l sister. I'a swap her out for you."

"Fuck you . . . Tell Roz buy some mo black clothes."

Duke hung up and clicked back over to the other line." Take care of it and meet me at the spot."

Shagg and Conrad met Hotboy and Duke in Kingsway Apartment. Word around town was that Will and his crew had set up shop out there. They were there to see it for themselves. Big A and Stunter saw the black Crown Victorias and thought that they were being busted by police but realized.

It was a hit-and-start shooting. Conrad's AR-15 sounded like church bells ringing. Shagg's gun jammed, and he tried to unjam it in the middle of the gunfight. Hotboy ran around the car and let out a burst of bullets. Big A took off running through the field when he ran out of bullets. Stunter was zigzagging across the field when Duke shot him, pushing his back through his chest. Shagg drove up on the grass.

"Let's go . . . let's go . . . let's go."

On the other side of town, Will's mom stepped out onto her back porch and had a heart attack. Her daughter was naked, badly beaten, hanging upside down from a dog chain. Half of her body was still submerged in the bucket of liquid fire, headfirst.

*   *   *   *

Chapter 18
Keeping It All Together

Duke didn't get to see La-La very much because of everything that was going on. When he popped up to her clothing store with roses to take her out to eat, she burst into tears. No matter what happened in the streets, Duke was a saint in her eyes. Whether he was selling drugs, tossing pennies, or pushing cans, La-La was going to support him. Deep down inside, she knew that he was a killer. The news was counting every body. La-La was just hoping that after he heard what she had to say, he would spend more time at home.

"Are you happy to see me?" he asked, reaching across the table to touch her face.

"You already know that I'm happy to see you. Have you talked to Roz lately?"

He knew that she had something to tell him because that was the only time that she asked about Aunt Roz.

"I haven't talk to her, but Shawn says that she is doing OK."

"Baby, I'm . . ." She started crying. "I'm three months pregnant . . . I'm sorry, I been wanting to tell you."

He came around the table to console her. Duke couldn't believe it—he was finally about to be a father.

"It's OK, we can just go shopping when I come home in the morning."

LaLa looked up with a smile on her face." You are too dam cool for your own good. How we gone go shopping, and I don't even know what I'm having yet."

"That don't matter. We gone buy boy and girl clothes. Whatever we don't use, you can give away."

"Baby, I gotta get back to the store," La-La said, looking at her watch. "We got two trucks coming in today, and you know I don't trust nobody but you with my money."

Two men wearing suits sat down at their table as Duke and La-La stood up to leave.

"What?" Duke asked, turning his nose up.

"You want to take a ride with us?"

"Am I under arrest?"

They looked back and forth from one another. "Nope, you're not."

"Well, leave me the fuck alone."

"We just want to know what you know about all of these bodies that have been piling up lately."

"I ain't got shit to say about no bodies." He dropped a card on the table. "Call my lawyer if you wanna talk," he told them, and they laughed.

"Well, we'll be in touch," they told Duke as they walked away.

Duke gave La-La his car keys when they got to the parking lot.

"Take my car and go back to work. Don't go home when you close up because I know that they gonna follow you. I want you to spend the night at Shawn's house, until I tell you that you can go home."

"Who was them people?"

"The feds."

*   *   *   *

Duke had lost so much to get the blessings that he was receiving the game had blessed him, but now he was wondering what was all of it really worth. No amount of money could bring Diron back, nor change the way that Aunt Roz felt about him. As he rode through Parkview on 30 inch Dubbrims, Duke felt like he was in a baby spaceship. Kids were running behind him, tapping the side of his Silverado. Duke pulled to the curb and gave away every twenty-dollar bill that he had in his pocket.

"All you gotta do is go to school, and you can be just like me," he said, watching them run off to the nearest candy store.

He saw the envious stares, but it didn't bother him. Over the years, he had tried to help everyone that he grew up with, but they were bad for business. They thought that hustling was about a new car and some rims. He made a U-turn, chunked the deuce, and kept rolling. Duke felt that it was time to give the game up, but how many hustlers knew when enough was enough? When he walked through the front door of his stash house, Duke couldn't believe that this was the new one. Every room was filled with trash bags full of fifty- and hundred-dollar bills. He couldn't have ever pictured himself to be in this position. Everything was happening so fast.

Someone always had their hand out. It was to the point that he didn't trust a soul, not even his own. Duke stashed the money in the secret compartments inside of the Ukon and drove it to Tina's house. She was on the phone when he walked in the door.

"Tell whoever that is you gone call them back later."

She hung the phone up. "Look what the cat drug in."

"I hope you gone be ready in the morning."

"You gone have to come get me because I'm going to the club tonight."

He hated dealing with Tina, but La-La was big pregnant, so right now he didn't have a choice. India and Tina were the only ones who knew the route. It would take forever to train someone else at such a short notice. Duke took his shoes off and sat down on the couch. Tina saw him dozing off and unzipped his pants.

"Let Moma give you some feel-good medicine."

He pushed Tina off of him and stood up. "Bitch, quit trying to seduce me all the time. Just be ready when I get here in the morning." He put his shoes back on. "Where the keys to my Lexus that's in yo garage?"

She looked at him with pure hatred in her heart. "They in my top drawer."

She watched Duke grab the keys and leave without another word. When Tina was sure that he was gone, she picked the phone back up.

"Hello."

"Hey baby."

"That nigga gone."

She propped her feet up to get comfortable. "Yep, that truck outside too."

"You sure that he be stashing the money in the truck?"

"We leave in the morning. I know what I'm talking about." The line went silent for a brief moment." Don't forget that you told me the same thing about the townhouse."

"Conrad, I know that it's there this time."

"I'm just being sure because I ain't tryna go on another one of your dummy missions."

Conrad gave Shagg the signal to put the other house phone to his ear.

"I know for a fact that it's there this time."

"You know I love yo freaky ass, huh. But daddy gotta go. Call me tomorrow and let me know what's the word."

"OK, love you too."

Conrad and Shagg sat back with million-dollar grins on their faces. For the past three years, they had been plotting to rob Duke. After Gwen was killed with his baby inside of her, he lost every ounce of love that he had for Duke. To them, Duke had been acting funny ever since Diron got killed. He didn't go to the club, come by their houses, or stop by Cent's house anymore.

"I told you that the bitch could set it up."

"Yea . . . yea, but why we can't just catch him by one of them hoes and rob him? We ain't gotta kill him. Let's just give him a leg wound or some shit."

"Just be patient, nigga. We gone hit this lick and then find out where he just moved to. I know that, that nigga got them Mils stashed at his crib."

"Well, we going to his house if ain't no money in this truck." Conrad shook his head. "Bet that up."

*   *   *   *

Big A and Rob were riding around looking at the huge houses in Will's neighborhood. A Benz truck and a Lexus were parked in the driveway, but the house looked deserted. Big A blew the horn, but no one came outside. He blew the horn again before getting out of the car. They beat on the front door but still didn't get an answer. He walked to the backyard and came back. Rob was about to knock on the door again, but Big A twisted the doorknob and found it unlocked.

"Something wrong, you know that this ain't like Will. You go check the top floors, and I'ma check the bottom half of the house," Big A told him, pulling out his gun.

The first room that Rob went in upstairs was a mess. He looked around and saw that the whole second floor was tore up. He was thinking the worst-case scenario when the whole third floor was also tore up. Big A got his attention by screaming at the top of his lungs. Rob ran back downstairs and found him sitting in the kitchen.

"Why they do him like this, dawg?"

Rob almost vomited everywhere when he saw what Big A was pointing at. "Ahh . . . ahh," he said, putting a hand over his mouth.

Will and Trina were sitting back-to-back in a high-back chair. They were bound together by duct tape around their midsection. Blood was still leaking out of the holes in their heads. Big A and Rob cried like babies seeing Will's brains all over the kitchen.

"We gotta call and get them some help."

Big A looked at Rob like he'd lost his mind. "Ain't nothing we can do."

"What, what do you mean ain't nothing we can do?"

Big A put his arm around Rob's neck. "Look at this shit, what . . . you gone call the police." He turned to Rob so that they were facing the two bodies. "All we can do is get all the dope and money out the house."

"How we supposed to do that?"

*   *   *   *   *

Duke sent Hotboy to pick up Tina and lay up at the Marriot with Daysha. She was all over him before they could even get the door closed. Duke was always rough with her, and she loved every minute of it. He hit her from behind, choked her, and pulled her hair at the same time.

"Harder . . . harder . . . harder, yes . . . ooh baby . . . right there, yes."

She made a million crazy sounds and told him to fuck her harder and harder. Duke laid pipe on her until the sun was peeping through the drapes on the window. Just as he was dozing off, his business phone vibrated.

"Hello," he answered in a sleepy voice.

"Where are you?"

"It's ready, just take the truck. I'ma get some shut-eye and catch a late flight."

Dre breathed a heavy sigh." Duke, I like you, but don't ever play with my money. I have been sitting at this house for over an hour, and there is no truck in this driveway."

He pushed Daysha off his chest and sat up, his mind was racing. Horns were growing from his head as thoughts started racing through his mind. Six million dollars. He threw the covers back and jumped up to put his clothes on.

"I'm on my way."

Things just went to shit from sugar, and he knew that this was only the beginning.

"Hello," a sweet voice said.

"Meet me at Tina's spot in twenty minutes."

"You know I gotta be at work in a hour."

"Shorty, just do what the fuck I tell you to do."

Who knew my truck was over Tina's house. Why was I stupid enough to leave my shit there overnight, he thought to himself. Hotboy pulled in behind him, and they walked into the house together.

"When I came home, yo truck was gone. I thought that you had it."

Duke slapped the taste out of her mouth before she could say another word.

"Bitch, don't speak unless you spoken to. Hotboy, what time you bought this hoe home last night."

"I don't know, 4:00 or 5:00 a.m."

Dre sat back puffing on a Cuban cigar. He was trying to figure out if Duke was acting or serious. Over the years, they had been doing flawless business—he had to at least give Duke the benefit of a doubt.

"You say you ain't see my truck outside when you pulled up."

"I wasn't paying attention but I don't remember seeing no truck. Better yet, I know wasn't no truck in the driveway because I pull all the way up."

Shorty walked through the front door and could tell something was wrong. The look on everyone's face said it all.

"Shorty, call the police and report my truck stolen."

She started laughing. "I know you ain't trying to scam the insurance people."

"Bitch, I don't see a muthafucking thing funny. Just do what I tell you for once in yo stupid-ass life."

Shorty's eyes watered up. "Why you mad at me, I didn't do whatever is wrong?"

Duke shook his head. "Just do what I said and call me."

"I'ma call the insurance people and call—"

Duke and Dre left together without another word being said.

*   *   *   *

"Hello."

"Sis, Roz OK?"

"She doing better, but she really ready to come home. She said that she don't know why she gotta be hiding out because you having problems in the dope game."

Duke bit down on his bottom lip. "Sis, shit looking bad for li'l bro. I just took a loss for 6 million dollars." He took a long drag on the blunt. "I need you to come home and get all of my money. I need my money to be with someone that I can trust. I got the money to pay these people, but they still might kill me anyway."

"You own all of this shit and you want quit. You have millions on top of millions, and you want walk away? Why the fuck you want just leave the game alone."

"I'm through," he pleaded before being cut off.

"I love you, but you gotta get yo shit together. Bye."

Duke closed the suitcases filled with money and drove to the airport. Dre was sitting in a chair, waiting for his flight, when Duke walked up.

"Today must be a special day or something?" he asked when Duke sat down beside him.

"I guess so, but it don't work that way all of the time."

"So did you take care of your problems?"

He looked down at the two suitcases, and Dre nodded his head.

"I'm not broke, but I do have to take unnecessary losses."

Dre started laughing. "Ooh, I know that you not broke. If my calculation is correct, you have more money than me. You know."

He glanced around to make sure that no one was eavesdropping on their conversation. "I don't like it, but I'll be sixty in a few weeks. You're only twenty-five years old. I wish I could go back to that age. You only live once. Duke. I can't keep telling you that. You have to enjoy the money that you are risking your life for." Dre slid a set of keys across the table to him. "You never know when your time is up—"

"I been doing some thinking, you know. I feel like my time is already up."

"Are you sure about what you say? Don't just feel like that because of what happened today. I need to know that you are serious."

He looked Dre straight in the eyes. "I'm positive, this is it for me."

Dre said something to his wife, and she walked away from the table.

"Can I send someone down here since you are retiring?"

"Nope, can't let you do that. I'ma talk it over with my crew and let you know what's up."

He gave Duke a smile and nodded his head, but Duke knew better. Dre would ruin the drug trade in Louisiana if Duke let him—that would only happen over Duke's dead body. A few minutes later, Dre's flight was called, and he stood up to leave.

"Call me if you ever need anything, and I do mean anything. You are the son I never had."

He gave Duke a hug and a kiss on the forehead before walking away. Duke walked away from Dre and the dope game, a very rich young man.

*   *   *   *

The Jolly Rancher–green candy paint was literally dripping onto the ground when Duke pulled into the parking lot of show cars. With 28-inch Dalvin rims dipped in gold, black Armani carpet, interior, and ragtop. His Regal was definitely a showstopper. Smokey the Bear would most likely be mad about all of the lumber on the inside of the car. After two years of waiting, it was finally finished. Hotboy couldn't believe that he was looking at the same car.

"That can't be yo Regal."

Duke smiled before hopping out of the car. A balding white man walked up and extended his hand.

"You must be Mr. Wright."

"Yep, that would be me."

He turned to the Regal. "Well, I can see that you like her. She truly is a beauty. The engine is chrome, top to bottom."

He pulled a remote out of his pocket, and the car came to life. The music came on loud and clear.

"Watch this."

He pressed the keypad, and the Lamborghini doors came up.

"Hell yea, das what I'm talking about." Duke tossed him a stack of money. "I fuck with you another time." He nodded his head and walked back toward the building. Duke put "Me and my Brothas" by Momason Ent in the disk changer and pulled into traffic. Necks were catching a crook as they passed by, running red lights like the streets were his. It had been a long time since Duke had that feeling, that shining feeling. The same feeling that made him stand out from everyone else around the city.

"The game done got salty, my nigga." He passed the blunt

"You know, they been on my ass for the past eighteen months or some shit."

"Why you want just retire and stop hustling. Shid, move out of States some shit. You got plenty of money, plus all the shit you got yo hands in."

"I'm through wit the game, I really mean it when I say it this time."

Shamekia and Precious were sitting outside Shamekia's building when he drove past the mailboxes. He backed the car in and let the windows down. Smoke rushed out.

"Girl, I know he didn't," Precious whispered to Shamekia when she saw BMN light up inside his trunk.

Back in the days, they were laughing at him, but now you were only laughing if you were on his team. Duke gave people a reason to hate him, envy him, and a dam good reason to be like him.

"Turn that shit down," Shamekia demanded, walking up to his car. "You shaking these dam walls."

Him and Hotboy got out and went in the building. "We ain't gon be long."

"Still, you need to turn that shit down."

He gave Hotboy the duffel bag and walked over to Shamekia. "What up there to eat, while you worring about some dam music."

"This." She pointed between her legs. "Don't eat it all at one time."

He pressed the keypad in his hand and watched the doors close, windows rise, and the trunk ease shut.

"Unt-uhh," Shamekia hollered behind him, "you and this hot-ass car finna get the hell away from me."

*   *   *   *

La-La rushed Duke as soon as he unlocked the front door. She wrap both arms around his neck and squeeze so tight that he thought she would strangle him.

"Whoa . . . whoa . . . I can see that you miss me," he said, picking her up off of her feet.

"I thought that something had happened to you. Aunt Roz said that you came down there and left the same day."

He rubbed his hand over La-La's basketball-shaped stomach. It had been six weeks since the last time that she had seen him. She was always sound asleep whenever he snuck in and out of the house. Her face, feet, and breasts were huge. Yet she was still the most beautiful woman that he knew.

"You getting so dam big." He ran his hand across her face. "I'm sorry for not calling you, but I had to take care of a few problems."

She looked deep in his eyes. "What's wrong?"

"I lost some money . . . let's talk about something else. How you been?"

LaLa slid her hand under his shirt. "I'm horny, I been waiting on you to come home." She ran her hand up and down his six-pack. "You bought me this 2.2-million-dollar home and haunt spent one night in it. I don't know if I be tripping or what, but I be hearing shit all the time."

"Well, I'm home now."

La-La took her nightgown off and took a step back so he could stand up. You couldn't really tell that La-La was 7seven months pregnant because she worked out every day. Duke unhooked his belt buckle, and his pants fell to the floor.

"You gotta catch the cat if you really want it," she told him and took off running down the long hallway.

As soon as he walked through the bedroom door, LaLa pushed Duke back onto the bed. She stood over him and began kissing down his stomach, making her way down between his legs. She opened her mouth to please him, but he grabbed the back of her head.

"No!" he told her, rising up off of the bed.

La-La was the only woman who hadn't pleased him orally, and he planned to keep it that way. He could get the best lip service in the world when he was in the streets, so he didn't need it at home. He lay on the bed for a moment before slowly climbing on top of La-La.

"Baby," she moaned, "be gentle. We might hurt the baby."

He kissed circles around her stomach. "Shush."

Duke took his time and gave her slow, deep, and long strokes of passion. LaLa met every stroke with her wide and luscious hips.

Ahh . . . ahh . . . ahh . . . baby, you . . . I . . . love . . . yoou . . ."

Duke was glad that they didn't have neighbors, because someone would swear that he was trying to kill her. Truth be told, he was most definitely changing her for all of the problems that he was going through. After what seemed like forever, Duke came in a burst of flames. La-La's whole body shook as the hot semen was being pumped into her body. Duke rolled over and lay down beside her. She laid her head on his chest and fell asleep.

*   *   *   *

"Tell that man what he wanna know about Duke and make that money."

"I just . . . you know."

Precious slapped Shamekia on the leg. "No, bitch, I don't know. Enlighten me."

"Regardless of what you say, you know that nigga my heart," she told Precious.

"Well, guess what . . . his girlfriend pregnant, and they say that nigga is a multimillionaire. Why, what you got?" She looked around Shamekia's apartment. "You gotta fixed-up project apartment and a 3 Series Beemer. What do you think La-La drives?" She grab a pen and a piece of paper. "She drives a Bentley coupe and lives in a million-dollar home somewhere. Now, I want you to weigh yo shit up next to hers."

She thought about what Precious was saying and realized that she was speaking the truth.

"Precious, that nigga take care of me, though. He pay all of my bills and put money in my pocket, what more can I ask for?"

"Fuck him," she hollered as she stood up. "That nigga sat right here in yo living room and collected a black hefty sack full of money. What, you got five grand . . . that's chump change. His people blowing that on a purse or a pair of shoes."

"Where that number at?" Shamekia asked, looking down at the floor.

"Here." She gave Shamekia the card. "That nigga don't love shit but his money. You better start doing the same, bitch."

*   *   *   *

"How you living, fam?"

"I'm chilling, why, what's up?"

Shagg grabbed the remote and sat down on the couch. "I'm tryna figure out a way to tell my gurl that I got Shanell pregnant."

"Shid, give her a present and break the news. Hold on right fast." Conrad moved the phone from his mouth. "Get the fuck out of my mouth and go in the living room." He put the phone back to his mouth. "Yea, I'm back."

"Don't kill her," Shagg told her, trying to muffle his laughter.

"Man, Tina is a nosy-ass broad."

"Peep, I'ma buy Pretty one of them Porsche trucks that we was looking at. What . . . you and yo gurl gone roll wit me."

"Me and my li'l mix broad gone go baby shopping in bout a hour, but I'a be ready about four."

"I ight, holla back."

Shagg put "Family First, The Motto" by Momason in the disk changer and rolled up a blunt. He couldn't come up with a good-enough solution to break the news to Pretty. This had his mind working overtime. He wasn't worried about her leaving because she was also pregnant. Most people said that he was crazy for messing with Pretty and Conrad had her first. *You can't help who you fall in love with. The heart doesn't have a mind,* he could hear her mouth. Conrad would be to blame. Pretty wouldn't be pregnant forever, though.

On the bright side, Conrad had helped him see the type of cash money that he had never seen before in his life. Since they started pulling capers off, money had been pouring in. Shagg bought fifty pieces of property and put away enough money to be set for life. That wasn't even counting the last lick for the 6 million dollars. Shagg wanted to tell Conrad that moving in with Tina wasn't a good idea, but he knew that Conrad wouldn't listen. He just kept quiet and let him do what he did.

* * * *

Duke jumped up when he heard his cell phone ringing. The clock on the nightstand beside the bed read 9:15 a.m.

"Yea," he answered, wiping the sleep from his eyes with the back of his hand.

"Wake up, sleepyhead." Shorty was hoping the news she had would make him feel better. "They found yo truck, baby."

He rolled over to La-La's side of the bed and saw she was gone. He knew where she was because he could smell the bacon in the air.

"Where it's at, you got it?"

"They say they found it in the back of Kingways."

"Have it dropped off at Mr. Atkins's shop and meet me up there."

He got out of bed, showered, and got dressed as quickly as possible. La-La knew that he was up when she heard the elevator chime.

"I'm almost finish with your breakfast." She turned around and saw that he was fully dressed. "Where you going, you just came home?"

"I just got a call about that money that I told you I lost. Put my food in the warmer and I'a eat it when I get back." He gave her a kiss on the lips and her stomach. "If you have some clothes on, when I come back, we can go baby shopping."

La-La wasn't happy to see him leave, but she understood the life that he lived. "Be careful."

"Always . . . always, baby gurl."

*　　*　　*　　*

"Where the fuck you been, and why you ain't return none of my calls?" Conrad closed the door and reclined his seat. "I told you that I was going to New York to meet them people who supply my stores. Shit, I just got back into town last night."

Duke looked deep in Conrad's eyes and didn't like what he saw. "Somebody stole my truck."

"What, where it was?" Conrad shot back, passing him a blunt to light.

"Where it was is not important. The funny thing is that my truck was only there for a few hours. It's like somebody was waiting to steal my shit," he said, staring at the heavy raindrops falling on his windshield.

"Fuck it, I know you got full coverage on all yo shit."

"The money that I owe the connect was in that fucking truck."

Duke pulled into the parking lot of show cars. The sight of his truck made Duke want to cry. Growing up, he had stolen some things, but it never amounted to much. In the game, you take losses, but Duke had never prepared for a loss like this one. Taking a loss for some dope was understandable, but losing 6 million dollars in cash was unheard of. The old saying that he always heard had finally come true. What goes around comes around.

"That can't be yo truck," Conrad said with a sly grin on his face.

Duke lit another blunt and let out a shallow laugh. "You know." He blew out a thick cloud of smoke. "If I don't quit hustling, I'ma kill everybody that I love, one way or another."

Shorty drove up and got out with a shocked expression on her face. "Baby, I'm sorry," she told him, looking at the burnt shell of a truck.

Bitch. I just lost 6 million dollars, and you holling about you sorry, he thought, looking at her and then the truck.

Conrad passed the blunt back to Duke. "Don't let that shit get you down. Let's go cop some new shit and show them that what don't kill us makes us stronger."

Duke didn't know if he was coming or going at that moment. He did know that Conrad was acting real strange, though.

Duke didn't know if it was the weed making him think that way or if it was his gut feeling, but something wasn't right. He let his head sit on the steering wheel to gather his thoughts. If he stay'd in Monroe one more day, he was going to kill someone.

"Conrad, take my car, and I'ma ride with Shorty. Tell everybody that I'ma call them later."

*   *   *   *

"I know I gotta wash my truck. We can't drive my shit, and it's dirty"

"Oh, so you just now noticing the wash-me signs."

Shanell gave Tina the middle finger through the mirror she was standing in.

"Is we still getting our hair and nails done today?"

"Yea, Conrad still gone let me get the Bentley. Since I know that that's what you asking."

Shanell put her skirt on and sat down beside Tina. "You know Will and Trina dead, huh?"

"I heard." Tina looked around the room like someone was listening. "I wonder where Duke at, though."

"You know what, I haven't seen him in a minute. Didn't he come get all of his stuff from out of your house."

Tina nodded her head and kept breaking up the weed.

"So"—Shanell was smiling—"how much they got out of that truck? Shagg wouldn't tell me, but I know you know."

"I don't know how much it was, but I know that it had to be a lot. Duke looked like he wanted to kill somebody."

"How much did you get?"

Tina licked the cigar close and lit the tip. "I don't, a hunit grand or so."

"Dam, no wonder why all the furniture trucks been going over yo house lately."

179

"Unt-unt." She had a mouthful of smoke. "Conrad paying for that shit," she said once she blew out the smoke.

"Go gurl, witcho bad ass."

* * * *

"Hello."

"Say . . . what up, where you at?"

"What up, Hotboy?"

"Peep this shit . . . Money, Tocky, Elmore, and Leroy got picked up by the feds." He took a deep breath. "Will and Trina dead too."

Duke sat up in bed. "What . . . you bullshitting."

"They say that Big A found them dead at the house in little Cuba."

"When this happen?"

"A few days after you left . . .So, what, I guess about three weeks ago."

"You mean to tell me that you—"

"Nah, nah, shid . . . I just found out about this last night."

"I'ma call you back."

As soon as his flight from the Bahamas touched down at Monroe Regional Airport, Duke collected his money off of the streets. He wasn't worried about selling dope anymore, because his money was long enough to last for generations. La-La was now bigger than a house and bound to go in labor at any moment. They were about to have an ultrasound but decided that they would let it be a surprise. Duke hadn't felt this good about being with a woman in his entire life. La-La put the S in the permanent smile plastered on his face. She didn't trip with him about nothing, and that made her the perfect match for him. Duke always said that he'd never get married, just a fuck here and there and then move on to the next one. He couldn't fix his mouth to say that he was leaving La-La.

Duke met with his team of lawyers to make sure that all of his businesses were running smooth. After his lawyers' office, he went to his dentist for an appointment. He had 20 karats' worth of diamonds put in his mouth. He wanted to get out and about, but his mouth was still numb. So instead, he went to his storage and pulled out the Viper. The first time that this car had been driven since the night that Diron died.

*   *   *   *

Chapter 19
When It All Falls Down

Conrad and Shagg were on their way to Parkview to meet up with Big A. They had been selling him dope for the past six months. He couldn't wait until Hotboy ran out of dope because then him and Shagg could make all the money.

"Man, you sho about this nigga? You already know I don't trust these nigga."

"Just chill. If you see something funny, start blasting."

Conrad backed the car up in front of the building beside Shamekia's building and looked around. Parkview was a big block party. People were moving about everywhere. Music was being played from the trunk of cars, and women in Daisy Dukes wandered about like chickens with their heads cut off. Conrad saw Diron's Viper sitting in front of Shamekia's building and Big A's Hummer parked on the grass. He checked the clip in the Mac-90, the extra clips, and reached out to pop the trunk. Shagg snapped the 200-round drum onto his AR-15.

"If I see some funny shit . . ." Shagg cocked the gun.

Conrad grabbed the duffel bag and walked toward Big A's Hummer. He was watching out for a surprise attack when he caught a glimpse of the look on Big A's face. Before he could turn around, Rob ran out from behind the building with an AK-47 in his hands.

"Bitch, don't move." He walked toward Conrad. "Drop the bag and I'ma give you a running start."

Conrad's mind started racing. He thought about all the people he killed, messed over, and wondered if he would be shot down in the projects. As hard as Duke strived to get them out of the projects, he was about to die there anyway. Everything froze in time. He didn't know whether to shoot or strike out running.

*   *   *   *

Duke lit the Purple Haze, and Hotboy pop the cork on the bottle of Louie XIIII. He had given Hotboy all of the dope he had left and was paid half up front. They had Shamekia's apartment jumping like a second line. Precious came through the door and immediately turned her nose up at him.

"Why you making my gurl shit hot and you got a house to go live in?"

"I ain't making a muthafucking thing hot. Ain't shit being sold up out of here."

She was about to say something smart, but someone knocked on the door. Duke grabbed the MP5 from under the table. "Who is it?"

"Baze and Lowdown."

Hotboy let them in, and Duke noticed that they were both wearing rubber boots.

"What's the deal?" he asked, giving them dap.

"Shid, me and Baze tryna get it. We gone need at least twenty apiece this time around."

"Dam', ya'll around finish."

They took the boots off, and he saw that the money was strapped to their legs, stuffed down inside of the boots. Precious's eyes got as big as bow dollars at the sight of all of the money they were piling upon the table. Duke pulled a small stack of money out of his pocket and tossed it to her.

"I need you to leave for a minute."

She put the money in her pocket and left without saying a word.

"How much this is?"

"Four hundred thousand, two hundred from me and two hundred from Baze."

Duke nodded his head. "This my dude, we call him Hotboy. He gone be the one who takes care of ya'll from now on. You can call the same number, but it'll be him who you'll talk to."

Lowdown looked from Duke to Hotboy and back to Duke. "Why we can't keep dealing with you?"

"You say ya'll want 20 birds apiece?" Hotboy asked, looking at Baze and Lowdown. "I'ma send somebody to pick you up in the morning. But let me tell you something about me. If yo don't pay me. I'ma kill you and him and bury you with the dope and money." He threw them a sack of Purple haze. "Smoke that and I'ma see you early in the morning."

Duke and Hotboy went downstairs, where Precious and Shamekia were standing around talking.

"Next time I tell you that I'm on my way, you better be yo ass there when I get there. I left you something on the table."

Precious pinched him on the arm. "Duke, you done blew the fuck up."

He gave her a devilish grin, and she put her hands over her eyes. "Boy, put the diamonds up, you blinding me."

They got in the car, and Duke dropped the top. He reached down to get the remote off the floorboard and heard someone scream, "Get the fuck down!" Gunshots rang out, and he fishtailed all the way out of Parkview.

*   *   *   *

Conrad dropped the duffel bag and ran for cover, shouting over his shoulder. Rob was aiming to kill as they marched toward the duffel bag. Shagg was holding court, but Conrad was trying to get out of dodge. Chopper bullets were breaking bricks into crumbs. Conrad was all over the ground, gators weren't meant for running. Conrad ducked in a building to load his last clip, and a shadow followed him. His heart dropped to the ground, and his gun flew up.

"It's me, nigga, don't shoot . . . Get the gun out my face," Shagg spat out, clutching the duffel bag.

"If we make it across the ditch, I'ma call Tina, and she gone come pick us up."

"I ain't got no mo bullets, and them niggaz steady shooting."

The sidings off of the buildings were all over the place. Red pieces of bricks were everywhere. Bullets were going straight through the apartments.

"I'ma start shooting, and we gone run for the gate. Let's go." Shagg got grazed on the arm and kept running. Their hearts were out running their bodies. Bullets sounded like missiles passing by.

Cha-cha-cha-cha-cha-cha-cha-cha-cha.

*   *   *   *

Duke was going 110 miles per hour leaving Parkview. Hotboy started rolling up another blunt to calm his nerves.

"Hello, who this is?"

"Tina."

"What the fuck you want?"

"Conrad and Shagg having a shootout in Parkview, and LaLa just went in labor."

"All right." He looked at Hotboy. "She having the baby, homie."

"Who?"

"La-La."

He pressed the gas pedal and weaved from lane to lane. He'd made a promise to La-La that he would be there when she delivered. She was one person that he didn't break a promise to.

He pulled into the emergency lane at the hospital and hopped out running.

"Sir, you can't park there," the security guard told them.

Duke kept running like he hadn't heard a word. Hotboy slid over into the driver's seat and found a parking spot. Duke ran up the stairs like his life depended on it. He was sweating and out of breath by the time he made it to the fifth floor. La-La was being pushed into the delivery room just as he walk through the door. He caught up with the doctor as he was going through the double doors.

"I'm that baby's father." He tried to catch his breath. "You just pushed her into that room."

He gave Duke gloves, a mask, hat, shoe covers, and a gown before he was allowed to enter the delivery room.

"Ooh . . . Get it out . . . Get it out" La-La screamed, bucking back and forth.

"Calm down, baby, I'm here."

La-La looked over at him and started crying. "Ooh . . . baby it hurts, it hurts."

"Mrs. Cole, we are going to need you to push on three, OK. One, two, three . . . push."

Duke's eyes got big as lightbulbs when he saw how big La-La's cat opened up. That brought his high all the way down.

"Excuse me, mister . . ."

"Mr. Wright."

"We are going to have to do a C-section. The baby is too big, and its turnt the wrong way. Ms. Cole has fainted, and we need to know how you think she would want to be cut."

Duke looked at him like he was crazy. "Dude, you done lost yo dam mind. I don't know, you the doctor."

"The bikini cut is the best because it leaves a small scar."

"Well, why you still standing here looking at me?" he asked, stepping back.

*   *   *   *

Conrad walked into the Baymont Hotel lobby, sliding his phone in his pocket. The lobby was empty except for the woman sitting behind the counter; her eyes were glued to a book. He shot a glance her way before walking up to the counter.

"What are you reading?"

"Oh, I'm sorry, what can I help you with?" she said in a panicky voice.

He stared at the caramel-skinned young lady. "Calm down, baby . . .uhm . . . let me get a suite."

Her hazel brown eyes me this. "For one night?"

"Baby, I'm the real thang, not a minute man. Make it a week.

She smiled, flossing her dimples and pearly whites. "Right now we only have two suites open. There is a boat race tomorrow, and we're kind of packed."

"Which one would you sleep in?"

She undressed him with her eyes before looking back at the ground. "The King suite, but it's too rich for my blood."

Conrad was admiring her perfect-fitting skirt showing off her curves in all the right places.

"Are you coming to see me, since that's the suite that I want?"

"Is that all I can do for you, sir?"

"Yea, that's it."

Conrad grabbed the key off of the counter and turned to walk away.

"Hey, you give up that easy."

"What you mean?"

"You ain't ask for my name or number, but you want me to come to your suite."

"I apologize. I got a lot on my mind right now. What is your name?"

"Yvette, what's yours?"

"Call me Conrad."

She wrote something on a piece of paper and stepped from around the counter to hand it to him. "Call me, a.s.a.p."

"Das what's up."

"I just might make that trip to the King suite when I let off."

"Dam, milk does a body good," he said, watching her walk away.

*   *   *   *

Duke didn't know if he could trust Conrad and Shagg anymore. Ever since his truck got stolen, they were always missing in action. Hotboy, Shagg, and Duke were sitting down, but Conrad was pacing the floor.

I'ma kill them niggas. Where ever I catch them niggas at it's over for them.

Duke walked over to him and pushed Conrad down to the loveseat. "You don't call no shots, that's my job. What I told you in the first place. Why you even selling that nigga dope, and where you get dope from? I know it ain't mine because I haven't given you shit in six months."

"I don't owe you no explanation for what I do. You don't call my shots."

Duke couldn't believe that Conrad was talking shit to him. Before he knew it, he slapped Conrad so hard that it could be heard in the lobby. Duke had sacrificed everything to see that the family wanted for nothing, and they repaid him by stabbing him in the back.

"I guess since ya'll got money, you don't need me no mo. Well, let me give you a piece of game. I know ya'll two stole my truck, but it's all good because every dog has its day. Conrad, you used Tina to pull it off, and I can't be mad because I slip. I'ma get all mine and some back, though. Everything you own is under one of my dummy corporations." Duke leaned back against the table. "All your accounts been froze and everything. Use some of that cash money you niggaz got stashed. I'm washing my hands. Oh yeah, call you a ride because a tow truck just came got that Range Rover and Bentley out of the parking lot. Hotboy, let's go."

*   *   *   *

La-La gave birth to Sha'kedria, a fifteen-pound baby girl. After being in labor for twenty-three hours, she had her tubes tied the moment that she pushed the baby out.

"That's it, no more kids for me," she said to Duke.

Duke was sitting in the chair beside the bed holding the baby. "Let's just have one mo."

"You better get one of yo skank hoes to push a baby out, because I'm not having no mo."

Duke was loving the feeling of being a father. His father wasn't there for him; he was planning on being the best father in the world. Conrad and Shagg left fifty cars on Shawn's street. It took a whole day to have them towed to Duke's warehouse. Shawn and Roz were finally able to come home since everything was back to normal. He had bought her a ten-bedroom, twelve-bath built from the ground up, but she refused to move.

Duke was sleeping on the couch when La-La woke him up. He hadn't been getting out much since she had the baby. His life consisted of baby shopping and family time.

"Baby," she said, tapping his shoulder.

"What, La-La?"

"I got the taste for some hamburgers."

Duke rolled over and sat up. "Go in the kitchen, make some hamburgers."

"It ain't no hamburger meat in there. You was supposed to go grocery shopping yesterday."

He looked at his phone. "It's after 12:00 a.m., La-La."

"I know." She stroked his face. "But that's what I wanna eat."

Duke knew that she wasn't going to take no for an answer. "OK . . . OK . . . OK. Dam."

*　　*　　*　　*

Duke turned off Highway 165 and pulled into a Wendy's parking lot. Stopping right in front of the big glass window. Cars went around him, blowing the horn. He was blocking the drive-thru. Duke was happy that they were still open because he didn't feel like driving all over town.

"Excuse me, sir." The cashier waved to get his attention. "You driving that car?"

"Let me get three number 2s, supersize, and I'ma go move it."

He walked away from the counter and went outside. Just as he was pulling off, a hail of bullets came from a black Monte Carlo. Duke grabbed the MP5 from under the seat and started shooting back. He hit the gas, ducking as he fled the scene. The vest that he had on was ripped.

He ran stop signs and sped through red lights, trying to make it back home. It took forever to make it to his street. He hit the brick mailbox and ran in to one of the garage doors. La-La heard the loud noise and came outside. Duke was lying on the ground beside the car.

"What happened? I'm sorry. Lord, please don't let him die. He too young," she said, seeing all the blood.

"I can't breathe, I'm dying," he told her, coughing up blood.

La-La put him back in the car, grabbed the baby out of the house, and fishtailed out of the driveway. She ran four red lights and a police officer got behind her, but she still didn't stop. La-La pulled into the emergency lane, got out, and the officer drew his gun on her.

"Get your fucking hands where I can see them."

La-La didn't pay him no mind. She was struggling trying to get Duke out of the car. Sha'kedria started screaming because she knew that something was wrong.

"He bleeding, please help me."

* * * *

Shagg, Tina, Conrad, and Shanell were sitting around Conrad's new house. He looked over at the wall monitor and dropped the blunt. Thirty men in black were running across his front lawn. He thought about grabbing his gun but changed his mind when he saw "ATF" on the back of one of the men's vest.

"ATF . . . DEA . . . FBI, get down, get down," they demanded, entering the house.

Conrad sat on the couch smoking his blunt. They slammed him down facefirst and cuffed him. Everyone else was already in cuffs.

Tina looked up from the floor. "Why they doing us like this?"

"Just be quiet. Don't worry about nothing. Man you got these fucking cuffs too tight."

"Where the warrants at, because ya'll got me fucked up. I know my rights."

A short man in plain clothes came through the door and gave him a piece of paper.

Conrad read the paper. "This bullshit, and you know it. I wanna talk to my lawyer."

The plainclothes agent opened up a manila folder. "The four of you have been indicted by the federal grand jury. For the murder of Katrina Rolls, William Burns, Shelia Burns, Manual Turner, Joe Turner, Regina Swann, Matthew Ranks, and Bobby Taylor. Also, conspiracy to murder for Clay-Bo-Jones, Monte Saint, and Stunter Wells. Oh yeah, someone just did a nice job on Duke."

Shanell started crying. "I'm pregnant, I don't know nothing about no murder."

"So you tryna tell me that all of those trips to Cancun, Jamaica, Costa Rica, and New York were from working a nine-to-five? I'm not even going to read you the rest of the charges because they are small compared to these."

Shagg shook his head in disbelief. This couldn't be happening. "Ya'll get the wrong people," he said, looking at the agent.

"It's about time you spoke up, Mr. Shagg. I'll cut you a deal right here right now. Testify against Conrad, and I'll promise you that you want get the death penalty."

"Bitch, do what you do."

"That's already done, Ms. Tina . . . is that you?" He knelt beside her. "I know Latasha wouldn't be happy if she knew all the things that you have done. She'll definitely find out if you don't help me, though."

"I didn't do nothing."

The short man looked around the room. "Get them out my face and tare this bitch up."

Chapter 20
I Still Can't Believe It

Shawn, La-La, and Hotboy were pacing the waiting room floor at St. Francis Medical Center. Duke had been in surgery for the past sixteen hours. He got shot in the arm, leg, hip, and in the chest six times. He was wearing a vest, but the kind of bullets that were used shredded the vest to pieces.

"Duke told me not to cry when he died." Shawn wiped the tears from her eyes. "That nigga left a couple hundred million stashed away. I don't know what I'ma do with all of this shit if he don't walk out of this surgery."

"Shawn, I got some money for Duke at the crib. You can pick it up when he leave here."

La-La was about to say something, but a doctor walked up with a piece of paper in his hand.

"I'm looking for the family of Kewhan Wright."

"Here we are," they said in unison.

"Could you come with me?"

They were walking down a long hallway when three men in suits cut them off. One of the men flashed a badge to the doctor.

"Could you tell me which ward Kewhan Wright is in?"

La-La remembered two of the men from Diron's restaurant.

"Why ya'll looking for my brother?" Shawn asked, eyeing the men.

"He's been indicted on twenty murders, ten counts of conspiracy to murder, and RICO."

La-La jumped in his face. "Ya'll always fucking with somebody. You know he ain't do that shit, but you still harassing him."

The doctor stepped between them. "I'm sorry to inform all of you, but Mr. Wright didn't make it out of surgery. He told me to give you this, Latasha." He held out the piece of paper to La-La and dropped his head.

???

Shawn broke down in tears. "Lord, I can't believe this boy??? died on me. La-La where that piece of paper that the doctor gave you?"

La-La dug in her purse and found the folded piece of paper. "Here it???" She wiped the tears from her eyes. "I can't even think straight right now. Shawn, I'ma need you to keep the baby for a li'l while."

"I'ma come get her stuff after the repass. Come on, read what the? te say."

La-La opened the piece of paper and read it aloud.

Hey Baby,

If you reading this I'm smoking a blunt with Diron and the rest of the homies. First of all, I wanna say that I'm sorry because this wasn't supposed to happen. I know you mad at me and you have every reason to be, I fucked up. But I gave you something that no one else has, Shakedria. When you see her you see me. I know I wasn't the best nigga in the world but I knew how to plan for the future. Tell Aunt Roz that I said I sorry, my life went down the drain when I let Diron get killed. I know you might not want to hear this but I split my love between two women. La-La, you was always number one and Shorty was my second. I left millions stashed in both of all garages because I love you. Shawn and Hotboy gone take care of the family. Shawn gone see that everybody get what they supposed to have, and I hope nobody gets mad. Tell Aunt Roz that I stashed millions to her attic, she deserves it and much more. Tell her to please except it. It's my last wishes. Now that I am dead and gone people can say what they want, but it has always been . . .

Familiar First, The Motto
2 B continued

Lightning Source UK Ltd.
Milton Keynes UK
UKHW041838260121
377731UK00008B/467/J